Cabin thirteen

"I hear you're quite the writer. Quite the teacher's pet."

"I . . . I don't know what you mean."

"No? Then maybe you're in for a surprise. And maybe it won't be a nice one."

The match hissed again. She saw his black, black eyes flickering.

"You should be more careful," Pearce said. "Anyone could find your key. Anyone could get into your cabin."

Kate whirled to face him. "I have a roommate. I'm not alone."

"A roommate?" And he sounded like he was smiling . . . a dark strange smile as if she'd said something peculiarly funny. "If someone wanted to get you," Peace said slowly, and another match went out, "a roommate wouldn't stop them. They'd just get you. Wouldn't they."

Other Point paperbacks
by Richie Tankersley Cusick:

April Fools
Trick or Treat
The Lifeguard

point

Richie Tankersley Cusick

SCHOLASTIC INC.
New York Toronto London Auckland Sydney

ISBN 0-590-43114-5

12 11 10 9 8 7 6 5 4 3 2 1 2 3 4 5/9

Printed in the U.S.A. 01

First Scholastic printing, December 1990

For Grandma . . .
your example has been the best teacher of all

Prologue

And so it ends, William.

At last.

I've never seen a dead body this close . . . at least not one still so warm.

And you made it so easy for me, too. . . .

By the time you heard me coming, it was already too late.

Just that sound you made when the axe came down . . . here . . . and here. . . .

Again . . . and again. . . .

Now there's just that strange look on your face.

Surprise?

Yes, surprise.

Surprise in your eyes.

Chapter 1

"I love to be scared," Kate insisted with a smile. "I'd love to write a book someday that would really terrify people." She paused on the top step of the train and shaded her green eyes from the late afternoon light.

"Oh, you young people and your obsession with horror! I bring you here for inspiration and meaningful prose, and all you want to do is hear blood-and-gore lectures by this William Drewe fellow!" Behind Kate, Miss Bunceton heaved her impressive bulk down onto solid ground and glanced around with a critical frown. "Well, honestly, I thought someone would be here to meet us! There doesn't seem to be a soul around!" She swung her suitcase to the platform and let out an exasperated sigh. "Just look at this place — it's like a ghost town! Take out your notebook, Kate; you can write a story about it."

Kate chuckled, one hand running absently through her short auburn hair. "Are you sure they're expecting us?"

"Of course. I called and made the reservations myself. Creative writing teacher from Webster High, I said, *and* my star pupil and writer extraordinaire, winner of our annual fiction competition — "

"Oh," Kate groaned, "you really didn't tell them that — "

"I most certainly did. Don't want them thinking we're small-town yokels." Miss Bunceton's eyes twinkled. "As long as you're getting a vacation from school, I want it to be an experience you'll never forget."

Kate smiled to herself. "They're probably just late. Come on, let's have a look around."

"You have a look, my dear." Miss Bunceton plopped down on a lopsided bench, regarding it with some dismay. "The train ride exhausted me. I've never had to go through so much trouble before just to get to a writers' conference. I should have chosen one *much* closer to home. Or farther south."

"It's cold here in the shade," Kate said. "Maybe you should go inside. . . . "

"Not in *that* thing." The woman looked suspiciously at the ramshackle building. "The roof will probably fall right down on my head. Go on and explore — I'll be perfectly fine."

Leaving Miss Bunceton to guard the bags, Kate wandered down the length of the platform, then circled the back of the building, trying to find a way in.

"Hello?" she called softly. "Is anyone here?"

As her ears strained through the silence, the

train whistle suddenly shrieked, and she jumped back, her body slamming into something warm and solid.

Whirling, Kate scrambled away from the silent stranger who stared down at her. He was tall, with hair and eyes as black as smoke, and as she struggled for composure, her anger burst out before she could stop it.

"Didn't you hear me calling? How long have you been there?"

His shrug was noncommittal. "You here for the conference?"

Kate regarded him for several minutes, mustering her dignity. "Yes. I was trying to find someone to help me. We just — "

"Where's your stuff?"

"Well . . . out in front, but it's not just me." She gave him a curious glance. "There's someone else with me." As she followed him around the building, she was relieved to see Miss Bunceton still keeping vigil with the luggage.

"Yeah, I know, it says here there's two of you." He shoved a piece of paper into his shirt pocket and strode on ahead. "Let me guess. Romance writers."

It was said with such obvious disdain that Kate felt herself stiffening. "What's wrong with romance writing? And anyway, I'm here to take classes with William Drewe — "

"William Drewe?" He threw a dark glance back over his shoulder. "I wouldn't count on that, if I were you. I'd get right back on the train and go home."

"Why? What do you mean?" She had to run to match his long, easy stride, and by the time she caught up she was out of breath.

"Oh, my dear boy, how *good* of you to make an appearance!" Miss Bunceton rolled her eyes at Kate and immediately began gathering up her things.

"He says I should go home," Kate said to her, and Miss Bunceton's look was equally bewildered.

"Go home? After all this inconvenience?" She gave a snort. "You must be *insane*."

"Look." The young man faced her, his jaw set in a mockery of a smile. "I'm just giving you the facts, lady, okay? William Drewe hasn't even shown up yet — in fact, he has a *habit* of not showing up for his classes. You probably won't even see him at this conference. Just a little free advice, that's all."

Miss Bunceton drew herself up and glared at him. "Well, we don't need your advice — and we don't need your help, whoever you are. Who *are* you, anyway? Kate, find us a taxi."

The black eyes seemed indifferent. "Pearce Cronan. And don't waste your time trying to find another ride to camp. I'm the only chauffeur you've got."

"Well, Pearce Cronan, I just might *report* you! What do you think of *that*?"

He waved one hand toward the train as the whistle sounded again. "I've got things to do. What'll it be?"

A shower of leaves whirled around them. As Kate looked into Pearce's deep eyes, a slow, cold shudder crept up her spine.

"Let's stay." She forced a smile and linked her arm through Miss Bunceton's, and they followed Pearce to his pickup, squeezing onto the seat beside him.

After half an hour of miserable silence, Kate was relieved to see the camp come into view at last. A thin gray fog floated through the trees as they drove past, smudging the shapes of cabins and darkening the thick autumn foliage. Pearce stopped the truck beside a large log building, then jumped out, piling their luggage in the dirt road.

"This is the lodge," he indicated with a nod. "And here," he dug into one hip pocket, pulling out another paper, "is a map. There's some kind of welcome party going on tonight — someone inside will tell you which cabin to use and when to eat." His eyes swept the tangled trees that crowded so close to the road. "Don't go wandering off the trails. It's easy to get lost in these woods. Things . . . anything . . . could happen." He hesitated, then glanced back at Kate. "Not for any reason. Got that?"

"We'll try to remember." Miss Bunceton sounded annoyed as Pearce ambled away. "Well, really, can you imagine? Not very considerate of William Drewe, hosting this thing and then not showing up. And you, so excited about his lectures — "

"He might still come," Kate said hastily. "Let's just go in and find out what we're supposed to do."

The lodge was bright and warm, with crowds of people milling about, sipping drinks, and munching snacks. Almost at once Miss Bunceton attached herself to a lively group, and Kate was relieved to escape unnoticed as she sought out a place to sit down. Spying a chair behind a potted plant, she collapsed into it, content to survey the gathering with droopy eyes. The long trip . . . Pearce's strange reception . . . and now here were all her classmates, all older than her, acting like they all knew each other, being so chatty and sophisticated. . . . She wished she could just find her cabin and sleep. She wished now she'd gotten back on the train when she'd had a chance.

With her eyelids almost closed, she suddenly started up and grabbed for the pinched spot on her arm. What she saw were two owlish gray eyes surrounded by steel-rimmed glasses, staring at her between the leaves of the potted plant.

"Psst!" hissed a voice that seemed to belong to the eyes. "Wanna escape?"

"Did you just pinch me?"

"Sorry. Didn't mean to pinch so hard," the voice hissed again. "If you fall asleep and someone sees you, you'll never forgive yourself."

Kate stared hard at the thick lenses and the oversized eyes. The leaves stirred, and a face came into focus . . . then a wide, boyish grin . . . and last of all, a head of curly brown hair crowned with a cowboy hat. The boy looked about thirteen, but his voice sounded older.

"You're right, I'd never live it down." Kate smiled, and the grin widened. A hand shot out through the branches and pumped hers warmly.

"Denzil Doyle. Seriously. Would I make up a name like that? And no, to answer your polite expression, I'm not a kid, I'm eighteen — but that means when I'm a hundred, I'll only look ninety-five or so. Come on. I'm gonna rescue you."

Giggling, Kate let herself be guided around the potted plant, and around another corner. Suddenly she found herself in a small, busy kitchen, face to face with her unlikely hero. He was small and slight, shorter than Kate and the other teenagers working around them, wrapped in a starched white chef's apron several sizes too big. She couldn't help but smile as that contagious grin lit up his face again and he gave a deep bow.

"Glad to be of service, ma'am. And you are — "

"Kate Rawlins." She smiled. "Thanks. I'm not really the socializing type."

"You don't seem like them," Denzil agreed. "So why're you here?"

"I won a fiction contest, so my teacher brought me with her to this conference — she thinks I can take back some good tips to share with the class. Also," Kate added modestly, "she thought it would inspire my own writing."

"Great! So you really *do* wanna be a writer! Me, too. It's my one art I suffer for — otherwise you'd never see me set foot in a kitchen." Turning toward a pantry, he sidestepped several workers carrying trays and tried to yell over a clatter of dishes. "Hey, Tawney, we've found us a soul mate! Oh, Kate" — his voice sank conspiratorily — "Tawney's okay, just a little — *you* know." He made circles with his finger alongside his head, then put his hands behind him and snapped to attention as a tall, pretty girl peeked out. "Tawney, this is Kate. She's one of us."

Tawney cocked her head, her long frosted hair curling damply around her flushed cheeks. "Hi! I'm Tawney!"

"She knows who you are. I just told her who you are." Denzil's glance was apologetic, and Kate hid a smile. "Tawney's into poetry."

"I want to be a poet." Tawney nodded. "I mean, I really want to write poems and things."

"But right now we have to refill these trays." Denzil gave her a little push and nodded at Kate. "Wanna help?"

"Sure. Can I sneak something to eat?"

"Sit here. I'll rustle up some grub. Relax. Enjoy."

Kate took the stool he offered and leaned over, resting her elbows on the countertop. As something brushed against her leg, she looked down to see a big black cat nuzzling her ankle and pawing lazily at her purse on the floor.

"Oh, that's Pet." Denzil glanced down at the cat and shoved a plate of cold cuts at Kate. "Original name, huh? She's the camp cat. Always hanging around. I think she really belongs to William Drewe, but he obviously never feeds her. Her name *should* be Pest. And you better watch out for her — she's a clothes thief."

"So I see." Kate laughed and rescued the scarf that Pet was slyly pulling from her open purse. The cat batted playfully at her fingers.

"She takes stuff and hides it — socks, gloves,

hats, shoes. . . . We find clothes all over camp. Even underwear." Denzil busied himself at the counter beside her. "Eat up. It's almost time for the bonfire. You're coming, right?"

"What bonfire?"

"So you haven't even looked at the schedule yet. No big deal. Just a way to welcome everyone. You can sit with us — now that we're old friends."

"Thanks." Kate swallowed a mouthful of cheese and watched Denzil slowly run a knife through a loaf of bread.

"So what are you here for? Romantic writing?"

"Horror."

"No kidding? Hope you're not disappointed."

"Oh, if you mean about William Drewe, I already heard." She kept her eyes on each deft slash of his knife. "Do you really think he won't be here? I just love his writing."

Denzil flipped his hat back from his forehead. "Know what I think?"

"What?"

"I think the guy had one too many drinks, and he's off in a stupor somewhere. Everyone knows he has a problem with the booze." Denzil gave a grin and went back to his slicing, and Kate leaned forward again, propping her chin on her hands.

"Do you know him?"

"Nah. Not really. I just work here when something's going on — retreats, conferences, stuff like that. And I can sit in on the lectures when I have free time. No one likes it when William Drewe's around — he's a real pain in the butt. Bossy. Really full of himself. Pearce lets the employees do their thing and doesn't hassle us."

"Pearce Cronan?"

"Right. The caretaker. The Drewes own the camp, but Pearce pretty much runs the show."

"So William Drewe lives here?"

"Yeah, the house is back in the woods, but it's off-limits to everyone. The guy's pretty antisocial when he's been drinking, I hear. Maybe even more antisocial than you."

Kate smiled. "What else do you know about him?"

"Hey, you really *do* have a writer's curiosity, don't you?" Denzil wiped his hands on his apron and handed Tawney a freshly stocked tray as she went by. "Bring the empty tray back this time, okay?" he reminded her, and then sighed as she gave him a dazzling smile and ran into the wall. "I'm not responsible, okay? If she causes a scene out there, it's entirely out of my hands."

Kate had to laugh, then rubbed wearily at her eyes. "I'm beat. I wish I knew who to talk to so I could go to my cabin."

"Cabin? Well, you're in luck, little lady. I just happen to have a guest list handy right — "

"Denzil?"

"What?"

"Let me guess. You want to write westerns."

He stopped, his jaw dropping. "Westerns! Heck, no, I'm a playwright! Heavy drama! Shakespearian theater!" As she giggled again, he worked his face into a stern gaze and peered over his glasses at a sheet of paper. "Now pay attention. *You* are in cabin thirteen with a Miss Naomi Bunceton — "

"That's my teacher, the one I was telling you about."

"Good. No strange roommates to get used to. However — you're in cabin thirteen. Which means you're in the very *last* cabin . . . *way* back in the woods."

"Oh, stop." Kate jumped to her feet as Denzil gave her a slow, smug smile. "You've been reading too many horror stories."

"I admit it." He nodded. "As many as I can get my hands on. I'm addicted. Here." He handed her a folder and motioned for her to open it. "This is the schedule. Breakfast starts at seven in the dining hall — that's where the main kitchen is — and it'll be served by yours truly. Any special diets, speak now or forever hold your palate. There's a list of classes, too, and a map — "

"I already have a map. Pearce gave us one on the way in."

"Ah, so you've met Pearce. The camp's resident zombie."

Kate had to smile at that. "He *doesn't* seem to be enjoying himself, does he?"

"Oh, you'll probably fall for him," Denzil tossed back, "so don't say anything you'll regret — "

"What are you talking about?" Kate laughed.

"Girls just do — fall for that type, I mean. The tall, dark, zombie type — "

"He's pretty strange," Kate said. "He warned us not to wander off the trails — made it sound almost scary."

Denzil considered this for a moment, then nodded. "Yeah, it *is* scary back in the woods. But why would you need to wander around, anyway? The trails take you everywhere — the lake if you wanna swim, canoes if you wanna cruise, stables if you wanna ride — " He glanced at his watch. "Whoops, time for the bonfire. Where's Tawney?"

Kate pointed as Tawney wandered back in, balancing an empty tray on each palm.

"You don't have to carry them like that when they're empty," Denzil hissed.

Tawney's eyes grew wide and serious. "I'm practicing!"

"Well, practice later." Denzil motioned to Kate as he headed out of the kitchen. "We're gonna be the last ones there."

"Okay, just let me empty this trash." Tawney hurried to the back door, tripping as the cat raced out between her feet. "Pet, get away from there, you're going to get all — oh, gross! What *is* that?"

"What?" Both the front room and the kitchen had emptied now; Kate let the door swing shut as she turned back around. "Tawney, is something wrong?" But when the other girl didn't answer, she frowned and made her way out onto the porch.

Tawney was on the bottom step, and over her shoulder Kate could see the cat. In the pale glow from the kitchen doorway, Pet hunched herself at the foot of the dumpster, her body as dark as the puddle all around her. She was licking something, her tongue making tiny quick sounds as she lapped at the spreading shadow on the ground.

"Tawney?"

As Kate stepped forward, she suddenly realized that the puddle around the cat wasn't a shadow at all, but something thick and wet that gleamed dully in the half light. As her gaze moved up the side of the trash receptacle, she could see a long, dark stream of liquid that spilled from the pile of garbage inside. . . .

From one large, oblong trash bag.

"Ooh." Tawney made a face and reached for the bag. "Someone must've thrown out some spoiled meat or something — only I don't smell anything spoiled, do you? And this bag's pretty big for — "

"Don't touch it," Kate said sharply, and Tawney looked at her in surprise, her hand stopping inches from the bag.

"But, Kate, the blood's leaking, and I have to — "

"Don't." Kate's voice was hoarse, and a strange, violent chill went through her. "Don't touch it."

She stared at the cat, and Pet looked up at them . . . her eyes widening . . . her whiskers glistening and wet.

Chapter 2

"Yeah? So what did it do?" Denzil tried to keep a straight face as Tawney's eyes grew wider.

"Well, it didn't do anything," Tawney replied seriously. "It just laid there and looked like garbage and kind of dripped."

"Ohhhh . . . " Denzil gave an exaggerated shudder. "Sounds pretty dangerous to me. Good thing you guys got outta there fast."

"It's not funny," Kate said. She was surprised at the sternness of her voice, and she dropped her eyes as Denzil and Tawney stared at her. "I mean . . . it didn't seem funny at the time. It was . . ." She shook her head, unable to put her eerie feeling into words. "The cat," she finished lamely. "She just sat there, eating it — "

"Cats are disgusting," Denzil agreed. "At least, Pet is. She'll eat anything. She has no pride at all."

Kate, staring hard into the flames, scarcely heard him. The three of them were pressed together in the flickering darkness, part of the human chain that encircled the raging bonfire. Around them people laughed and shoved good-naturedly, roasted marshmallows and shared new friendships, while Kate huddled there, feeling like an alien. That scene back at the dumpster had upset her; she didn't understand her foreboding, and now she felt silly. Beside her, Denzil skewered a fat marshmallow onto the end of her stick and gave her a wink.

"Congratulations, you've probably stumbled onto something really important. The Garbage That Ate the Writers' Conference."

In spite of her mood, Kate laughed. "Why do I get the feeling you're impossible?"

"Has my reputation preceded me?" Denzil feigned surprise. "Has Tawney been telling you how notorious I am?"

On his other side Tawney turned her attention back to them. "I never said you were glorious. Who's ever heard of that, anyway, a person being glorious — "

"Forget it," Denzil chuckled, exchanging amused looks with Kate. "I think they're telling ghost stories — let's listen."

Around the fire, the chatter began to die down as someone launched into a tale about a haunted house. Kate pulled her knees up to her chest, trying to concentrate. Against a backdrop of night-black, tongues of scarlet and orange licked hungrily at the shadows, distorting the faces around her, macabre demons with twisted grins and maniacal eyes. Kate shut her own eyes and listened as the ghost story ended and another began. This one was about doomed campers and a psychopathic murderer with a twelve-inch knife. From the shifting shadows, voices whispered and gasped, bodies moved closer together in fear and anticipation. I love to be scared, Kate reminded herself. *What's the matter with me? I'm supposed to be having fun. . . .*

"I know one," Denzil spoke up so suddenly that she jumped. She opened her eyes in time to see him push the brim of his hat back from his forehead and scan the crowd to make sure he had everyone's undivided attention. "There were these kids out parking," he began, and everyone groaned. "No, wait, this is really good!" The mumbling sounds subsided, and he started again. "And they heard on the car radio that this crazy guy had escaped from a mental institution — "

"I've heard this one," Tawney hissed.

"*Anyway,* they heard something scratching at the car door . . ." He paused dramatically. "And then . . . the guy stepped on the gas . . . and then — "

"You're telling it wrong," Tawney hissed again.

"And *then,*" Denzil said firmly, ignoring the snickers from the crowd, "when they got home and opened the door, this bloody *hand* was *hanging* from the door — "

"That's old!" someone laughed, while others joined in.

"Not *that* old." Denzil grinned.

"*Old.*" Kate nodded. "And anyway — "

"It wasn't a hand," someone else called out. "It was a hook!"

"Hey!" Denzil shouted back, his grin widening. "It was a *hand*! A *severed hand*!"

"It was a *hook*, Denzil." Kate cracked up at his innocent expression.

"I told you you were doing it wrong," Tawney said. "Did you make that up?"

Denzil stared at her, shaking his head. "Is a brick thick?"

"A brick?" Tawney's look turned thoughtful. "What does that have to do with a severed hand?"

"A hook," Denzil corrected. "You're telling it wrong."

"I am?"

"You *are* impossible." Kate jabbed Denzil in the ribs.

"Thanks."

"But if you don't mind, I'd really like to turn in. I'm so tired."

"I reckon you can be excused, little lady." Denzil gave a slow drawl and helped her up. "Need a hand findin' your bunk? I just happen to have your key right handy — grabbed it on the way over."

Kate looked surprised. "You did?"

"Sure. They were handing them out in the lodge. Yours was the only one left."

"Oh . . . then do you mind?"

"My pleasure, ma'am. Tawney, I'll be back — gonna take Kate to her cabin."

" 'Night." Tawney waved. "See you at breakfast."

Denzil draped one arm across Kate's shoulder,

steering her away from the bonfire and onto a path that wound back through the woods. The cold silence was almost a shock as they went deeper into the night. Overhead, a biting wind swept black clouds across the moon, and Denzil switched on his flashlight. Kate shivered as he played the light over her face.

"I know. Kinda creepy out here."

"I like to be scared. Anyway, I'm just cold," Kate said quickly. "And I just remembered I don't have my suitcase."

"It should already be in your cabin. Pearce is in charge of all that." He held back a low branch for her to duck under, and the beam of light arced out before them. "Here we are. I'll just make sure everything works before I leave."

As Denzil fumbled the key into the lock, Kate glanced uneasily behind her. Leaves rattled softly across the path, and from some hidden corner of the woods a tree branch groaned.

"Well, the lights work. So far, so good." Denzil held the door and motioned with his free hand. "Small and cozy. Just think of it as your friendly, back-to-nature kind of place."

"It's nice." Kate nodded. "I like it."

"Great. We aim to please. I'll just start this heater for you, and now," Denzil paused in the doorway. "I'll be moseyin' along. Sleep tight, don't let the fleas bite, or whatever the hell these little critters are out here."

"Thanks." Kate smiled.

"Sure thing. Lock up behind me, and enjoy the conference."

"I'm sure I will. Good night."

She stood on the porch and watched until the beam of his flashlight had been swallowed by the darkness. It was quiet . . . as if she were totally cut off from the rest of the world. *Cut off . . . like that hand on the car door. . . .*

"Hook," she whispered to herself. "A hook . . . not a severed hand."

Something stirred the leaves at the side of the path.

Uneasily she opened the door and started back in. . . .

And heard a soft whisper behind her.

"*Kate. . . .* "

Spinning around, Kate's eyes searched the shadows, her hands clenched at her throat.

Nothing moved. Everything, deadly still.

"Hello?" Kate called. "Is someone there?"

A faint breeze fanned the forest, tendrils of fog swirling at her feet.

Trembling, Kate slammed the door and locked it.

For a moment . . . just a moment . . . she thought she'd heard that whisper again. . . .

"*Kate . . . Kate. . . .* "

Chapter 3

"Why, I was absolutely starved! Must be this fresh woodland air." Miss Bunceton dabbed at her mouth with her napkin and heaved herself up from the table. "What about you, Kate? All geared for a creative day?"

Kate nodded, stifling a yawn. "Bring on the muses. I'm ready."

"Well, you don't look ready. Gracious, I hope my snoring didn't keep you awake last night."

Kate hid a smile and watched her teacher leave the noisy dining hall. She hadn't slept well, but it hadn't been Miss Bunceton's fault; her dreams had been full of whisperings and images of dripping blood. She pushed her uneaten food away and jumped as a hand came out of nowhere and slapped her wrist.

"Shame." Denzil stood over her in his grease-stained apron, trying his best to look stern while Tawney waved from behind his back. "Think of those poor starving children."

"Oh" — Tawney's eyes looked worried — "do you know some?"

Denzil shot her a patronizing look. "It's just an expression, Tawney. Something your mom would say."

"Oh." Tawney nodded, her permed hair bouncing eagerly around her face. "My mom never said that. I thought you really *knew* some starving children and — "

"Are you going to William Drewe's lecture this morning?" Denzil cut in, pulling up an empty chair beside Kate.

"Oh, you mean he came after all?"

"No, but someone's substituting for him, I just heard."

"Who?"

"Got me. But I can think of a million people I'd rather listen to than him."

"You really don't like him, do you?"

"I told you, he's a jerk. Anyway, Tawney and I don't have to clean up this morning, so I'll join you, if that's okay. She has some poetry reading to go to."

"I'd love it. I'm feeling like a real outsider."

Denzil nodded, taking in the room and its occupants. "It's always like this at first. Once you get into the lectures, people'll be easier to talk to. But why worry? You have me."

Kate smiled. "*That* was certainly worth coming for."

"You bet. See you in a few minutes."

"Denzil — "

"What?"

"Did you come back to my cabin last night?"

He looked blank, shaking his head. "No. Why?"

"Oh, nothing." Kate shrugged uneasily. "I thought I heard something, but I must have imagined it."

Denzil gave a wise nod. "Inspiration calling. Did you answer?"

"No, I ran inside and locked the door."

"Too bad. Guess you'll have writer's block all day."

Kate felt a little better as she made her way to her first lecture. She found an empty chair, smiling back as several people looked up from their notebooks to say good morning. All around her she could hear speculations as to who William Drewe's replacement would be.

People were still chatting among themselves when the young man walked into the cabin. Alone in her corner, Kate noticed him at once as he pulled the door shut behind him and paused for a moment to check the time on his pocket watch. He wore jeans and a bulky knit sweater the exact color of his violet eyes, and light brown hair fell stubbornly over his forehead even as he gave it an absentminded swipe with one hand. As Kate tried to study him without being obvious, he began making his way slowly through the room. She glanced at the empty chair beside her, then up again as he passed it by and went to the podium in front. Placing some papers on the table, he calmly surveyed the room, not appearing to notice when the door opened and closed again and a breathless Denzil slid into the seat beside Kate.

"Good morning," the young man said quietly. His soft features and long-fringed lashes gave him a look of shyness, yet his voice sounded poised and self-assured. He stood relaxed, hands in pockets, and after a moment's hesitation, spoke again. "My name is Gideon Drewe. I know that all of you were expecting William to lecture here this morning, but due to unforeseen circumstances, I'm afraid I'll have to do."

There were shuffles and shifting. Kate saw looks of open curiosity around the room.

"William is my brother," Gideon said. A general murmur of surprise rose around him, but he seemed quite unperturbed. "For all you skeptics, let me reassure you that I am, indeed, a writer, though not as well known to you as William is. We've consulted together on his work, and I'm very familiar with his teaching methods. I hope you won't be disappointed." A faint smile flickered over his face, and once more he looked slowly over the room. "Since you're all here because you enjoy being frightened, let me just say this. Fear is a personal perception. And we can control our fears to some extent by writing about them."

"He doesn't seem upset," Kate mumbled. "Do you think William's okay?"

"Who cares?" Denzil whispered back.

"How old do you think he is? This guy, I mean. Does he look old enough to be teaching this class?"

"Old enough? Do you teach better if you're old?" Denzil leaned over, still trying to keep his voice down. "Early twenties, I think. He writes short stories. Thrillers. He's been published in lots of magazines."

Kate looked at him in surprise. "How do you know that?"

"I know lots of stuff." Denzil grinned. "He lives upstate somewhere. Why are you so interested, anyway?"

Kate held her finger to her lips as Gideon's eyes began another sweep of the room. This time as they passed over her, they flicked back, settling softly on her face, staying there so long that she began to blush. They moved away.

"Fear," Gideon was saying, his voice soothing, confident. "What frightens one person may be totally unthreatening and unimportant to someone else. Fear is in the mind of the beholder."

"What kind of accent does he have?" Kate whispered. "Is it British? It sounds kind of British — "

"It's culture," Denzil responded dryly. "It's the accent guys use when they think they're great literary geniuses — "

"Ssh!" Kate scribbled Gideon's words into her notebook. The room was silent, except for pens on paper, and the smooth spell of Gideon's voice.

"Fear can distort our impressions," Gideon said. He crossed slowly to the window and stood with his back to them, gazing out at the rainbow of fall colors and the patches of crystal-clear sky. "I love autumn.

I love children and animals. And kindnesses make me cry."

As every eye settled on him in unspoken empathy, he suddenly turned around, his startling eyes full on Kate.

"Perhaps William is dead," he said softly. "Perhaps . . . I killed him."

For a moment there was shocked silence. A gasp of surprise. And then . . . wary looks and an undercurrent of mutterings.

"So you see," Gideon went on, moving back to the podium, "now your whole perception of me has changed. You're wondering what really happened to William and if I really did have something to do with it. You're wondering if I'm a murderer. You're wondering if I'm a compulsive liar. You're wondering," and his eyes slid over Kate, "if I'm going to kill you, too." His gaze lingered on her again, and then a slow, faint smile spread over his face. "And that, ladies and gentlemen, is manipulation. As a writer, you can manipulate your reader with fear, just as I've manipulated you this morning."

There was a relieved burst of laughter; several people clapped. Tension gave way to warm camaraderie as people looked from one to the other, sharing the joke. Kate glanced at Denzil, who was shaking his head suspiciously.

"He's wonderful," Kate whispered.

"He's nuts."

"And so," Gideon continued, "in this class, hopefully, we'll learn to use fear to our advantage. If you have any questions, please ask. And for those of you who sent manuscripts ahead to be critiqued, I have them here, and I'll be glad to set up a meeting with you. Let's see . . . Rick Dennison . . . Mary Jackson . . . Lise Scheering . . . Kate Rawlins — "

"Me?" Without thinking, Kate's head came up from her notebook, her voice rising in disbelief. "Excuse me, there must be some mistake — "

Gideon looked from Kate to a bunch of papers in his hand, his expression equally puzzled. "Kate Rawlins? A short story, let's see . . . 'Dark Surprises'?"

Kate felt her cheeks burning as people began to turn and stare. "Yes, that's mine, but I didn't send it — "

"No, actually it was submitted by a Naomi Bunceton — "

"Oh, no, my teacher!" As laughter burst around her, Kate saw Gideon's amused smile, and she sank back, wanting to disappear. Even Denzil seemed to be enjoying the joke.

"All right then, just stay a few minutes after, if you can, and we'll talk. And don't look so worried, Miss Rawlins, your story was excellent," Gideon said. And then to the class, "Before we go any further, let's consider for a moment where a writer gets ideas, shall we? By the end of this conference, hopefully we'll have explored lots of methods to generate fear."

The hour passed before she even realized it, and it was with reluctance that Kate finally closed her notebook and gathered her things. Denzil was reviewing the notes he'd taken and didn't notice that Kate was ready to leave until she tapped him on the arm for a second time.

"You can't say he's not wonderful," Kate teased him. "You're as fascinated as I am."

"He was okay," Denzil conceded. "Just okay. I've heard better lectures that — uh-oh, here he comes. Put on your armor."

"My armor? What are you talking about?"

"I know that look." Denzil scowled. "And Gideon Drewe hasn't kept it off you all through class."

Flustered, Kate whirled around to find Gideon behind her, his hands clasped at his back as he waited politely for their conversation to end.

"Ah, Miss Rawlins. Do you have a moment?"

"Well . . . I . . ."

"You're on your own, kid." Denzil patted her shoulder. "See you at lunch."

"Wait — but — "

"This won't take long," Gideon said, watching Denzil go out the door. "If you're on your way to another lecture now — "

"No, that's okay." Kate settled herself in a chair and looked up at Gideon towering over her. He was holding some papers, and as he sat down, she saw a title on the top page and realized it was her short story. Gideon caught her glint of recognition, smiling as she looked away.

"You're uncomfortable with my having this, aren't you?"

"I didn't know Miss Bunceton sent it in," Kate said evasively, then sighed. "Yes. Very uncomfortable."

A warm smile spread over Gideon's face. "You shouldn't be. It's very good."

Kate's glance was shy but curious. "Really?"

"Really. As a matter of fact, I read all the submissions that William received, and I was very impressed with your talent. I feel you have great potential."

"Well . . . I . . ." Kate didn't know what to say, pleasure and embarrassment making her tongue-tied. "What I mean is, I've always wanted to be a writer. So that means a lot, that you think it's good." *God, I sound just like Tawney —*

"Thank you, Kate. It's flattering for one's opinion to be held in such esteem." Gideon's smile widened. "But you have to believe in yourself, too. Do you believe in yourself? In your dreams?"

Kate thought a moment. "Yes. I've never wanted to be anything else."

"Then what a head start you have. You see, these conferences aren't just for building the talent — they're for building the ego, as well. Writers are a notoriously insecure lot."

"You don't seem insecure." Kate studied him, the striking color of his eyes, the serene expression on his face.

"Looks can be deceiving," Gideon said smoothly. "Just like fears. At any rate, I'd love to go over your work with you. Nothing formal. We'll just toss some ideas about."

"I'd like that."

"Say . . . tomorrow morning? About eight?"

"Sure. That'd be great."

"Eight . . . yes . . . eight would be great." A faint smile flickered across Gideon's face, then slowly faded, his voice drifting off to a whisper.

"Did I say something funny?"

"No. It just reminded me of something. Someone. I'm sorry."

"Well . . . tomorrow then." She started to get up, but his voice stopped her.

"I noticed you last night. I was hoping you'd be in my class."

Startled, Kate stared at him. "You noticed me? I don't think I saw you. . . ."

"No, of course not. It was at the bonfire. You were halfway round the circle." He turned slightly to peer out the window. "It's a lovely day. I hope you enjoy it."

As he offered his hand to help her up, Kate couldn't resist one more glance at his face. Surprised to see Gideon looking back at her so intently, she reached for her notebook and knocked it to the floor. As they both bent to retrieve it, the door suddenly opened and a shadow fell across the threshold. Kate jumped up, agonizingly conscious of Pearce's dark stare upon them.

"What is it?" Gideon asked, unperturbed. Kate grabbed up her notebook and groaned as her purse fell to the floor. Squatting to pick it up, she didn't have to see Pearce to know he was watching her — she could feel his eyes boring into her back.

"Clumsy," she mumbled. "Sorry." Knowing her cheeks were bright red, she backed toward the door, avoiding Gideon's eyes, maneuvering around Pearce's body. "I enjoyed the class — really — thanks a lot."

"My pleasure," Gideon said as he rose to his feet. He glanced at Pearce and then at her, his voice oddly distracted. "I look forward to teaching you quite a lot . . . about fear."

Chapter 4

"So what kind of propositions did he make?" Denzil whispered in Kate's ear as he set some crackers on the table.

"Will you stop?" Kate shook her head at him, laughing, and he backed away with a grin.

"Hey, trust me, I *know* his type — "

"He just wants to critique my story, that's *all*!"

"Right. Critique today, kiss tomorrow."

"Don't you have work to do?"

"Oh, so now I'm just a lowly busboy in your eyes — and here I was so sure you wouldn't be fickle!"

"Good heavens, what are you two jabbering about?" Miss Bunceton tried to talk around a mouthful of salad. "Is something wrong with your food, Kate? Who *is* this boy?"

"Denzil Doyle. And no, my food is fine." Kate swallowed a laugh as Denzil made a face behind Miss Bunceton's back and disappeared into the kitchen. "Did you enjoy your classes this morning?"

"I should say I did! Romantic heroes — titillating dialogue — and then the *best* discussion on love scenes! I tell you, Kate, I am just so *inspired*! What did *you* do, dear?"

"William Drewe's brother took over his class — and that was quite a surprise about my story being critiqued, Miss Bunceton."

Miss Bunceton chuckled and threw Kate a sly look. "I believe you'll thank me in the end, Kate. For taking the initiative, I mean. You're much too modest, my dear. And has anything been said about William? No one seems to know what's going on."

Kate's mind wandered back over Gideon's class, the magical spell of his voice, how she'd hung onto every word. He'd been such a commanding speaker, yet so softspoken, that when the lecture had ended, she'd felt like a dreamer slipping reluctantly from a sweet, enchanted sleep. *And he liked my story . . . he wants to talk to me* —

" — don't have to go to all the lectures, you know." Miss Bunceton broke into her reverie. "You're here to play, too. Join some activity, have a good time. Take advantage of this experience, Kate — good heavens, *I'll* never tell!"

"Yes . . . well . . ." Hurriedly Kate pulled out her schedule, disappointed to see that Gideon had no more lectures that day. "I want to go over my notes after lunch. And then I thought I could do some exploring this afternoon."

"Excellent idea. Just remember what that Pearce fellow said about going off the trails."

"Yes, I'll remember."

As soon as she'd eaten, Kate wandered into the

dining hall kitchen, finding a spot near the back door that was out of everyone's way. Tawney saw her and tried to wave, her arms full of freshly washed glasses, and Denzil made a mad dash as several of them slipped from her grasp.

"Don't even speak to her," he scolded Kate, swinging himself up onto the counter beside her. "She can't think about two things at the same time." As Kate gave him a chiding look, he grinned. "So the spell's broken? You're back down to earth? Fallen from the spell of Gideon Drewe?"

"Denzil, I told you — he's just a great teacher! I can learn a lot from him."

"I bet you can." He jerked away as Kate slapped at his arm. "Debonair Mister Drewe — that accent girls go crazy over — that genteel air — "

"Oh, I think he's so handsome." Tawney nodded eagerly as she walked up and stood between them. "I saw him this morning on the way to my lecture. I've seen him before, too, and he just gets handsomer every time. Don't you think so, Kate?"

"Course she does," Denzil said before Kate could answer. "She's the teacher's pet — she thinks he's God."

"Oh, Denzil, for heaven's sake — " Kate began, but Tawney cut her off.

"Teacher's pet? He had one this summer, too, didn't he?"

"Don't tell her that," Denzil snorted. "You'll break her heart!"

"You will *not* break my heart," Kate flared up. "And anyway, she just *thought* she was his pet.

It was pretty one-sided, if you ask me."

"What was one-sided?" Kate demanded. "Will you please tell me what you're talking about?"

"This past summer." Tawney sighed. "She worked with us here in the kitchen — Denzil, what was her name?"

"Merriam."

"Yes, and she *loved* Gideon! She was hopelessly, totally, passionately — "

"Will you just tell the story, Tawney? Jeez. . . ."

Tawney smiled sentimentally. " — in love with Gideon Drewe."

"Was he . . ." Kate tried hard to sound casual. "Was he in love with her?"

"Heck, no." Denzil scowled. "But you'd never have guessed it to hear *her* talk."

"She told everyone." Tawney nodded. "*Everyone.*"

"Said she and Gideon were gonna run away together. Everyone in the kitchen knew about it — "

"I wrote a poem about it, too. 'An Unlikely Pair and the Great Affair' — "

Everyone around *camp* knew about it — students, workers, delivery people, teachers — even Pearce. Everyone but Gideon."

Tawney looked at the floor, her face suddenly sad. "But maybe he *did* find out about it, Denzil. Maybe that's why she left."

At Kate's puzzled expression, Denzil added, "Nobody *really* knows what happened. She just didn't show up for work one day. When someone went to her cabin to check on her, all her things were gone. We figured she just split."

Tawney nodded solemnly. "We figured maybe they had a lover's quarrel. In fact, I wrote another poem — "

"Except Gideon seemed totally oblivious to the whole thing," Denzil added, ignoring Tawney.

Kate pondered the story, looking quizzically at Denzil. "Did anyone ever find out what happened to her?"

Tawney exchanged looks with Denzil and gave a half nod.

"So?" Kate looked from one to the other. "What?"

"They think it was suicide." Denzil gave her a wry smile. "Trust me — you don't wanna hear about it."

Kate opened her mouth to ask more, but Tawney jumped forward with a scream.

"Oh, my gosh — the dishwasher! I must have put in too much soap!"

In dismay they watched as a wave of suds surged across the floor. As everyone yelled and scurried for mops, Kate let herself quickly outside.

Breathing deeply of the crisp air, Kate hugged her notebook to her chest and started off for her cabin. The pathway was so beautiful today, with none of the threats that had hidden in last night's shadows. Overhead the trees entwined their scarlet and green plumage, filtering pale sunlight into freckles along the trail. Thinking of Gideon, a quick smile came to her lips, then faded as the conversation in the kitchen came back to her.

"Teacher's pet . . . trust me, you don't wanna hear about it."

Spying the cabin up ahead, Kate slowed, letting her gaze run appreciatively over the little clearing. Now she could see how the trees crowded in from all sides, obscuring practically everything but the porch.

Perfect place for someone to hide.

Surprised at the unexpected thought, Kate forced it away. *What's the matter with you? It's a gorgeous day, you just found out you're talented, your teacher is the best-looking guy you've ever met in your life —*

Something slithered against her foot, curling around her ankle.

With a scream, Kate jumped back against the wall. There was a quick streak of shadow, and two eyes blinked at her from beneath a bush by the path.

"Pet?" Cautiously Kate knelt down, hands extended. "It *is* you, isn't it? Poor kitty — come on — I didn't mean to scare you."

Playing hard to get, the cat regarded her with saucer eyes, her back hunching in annoyance as Kate came closer.

"Here, kitty. What's that you've got in your mouth? A glove?"

Chuckling, Kate squatted a few feet away and wiggled her fingers enticingly. The cat blinked and snaked its tail, then at last padded slowly and deliberately over, sitting smugly just out of Kate's reach.

"Naughty girl," Kate scolded gently, inching closer. "You *do* have someone's glove. And they're probably out there somewhere looking all over for it."

Pet's eyes grew rounder. They fixed on Kate with a strange glow.

"That's a good girl . . . just let me see what you've got now — "

And at first it didn't register, the glove so thick and bulky as she eased it from the cat's mouth, the faint spoiled odor that met her nostrils and the way the fingers should have flopped, empty fabric, only they didn't, and the sudden awful realization that what she was holding, what she was looking at, was solid, was —

"Oh, God — "

She saw the cuff of the glove, one horrible glimpse of stringy red meat and dull white bone, and as a cry bubbled up in her throat, the glove fell with a thud at her feet.

And then, as Kate screamed, the cat slid into the shadows and watched silently as Kate raced along the path toward camp.

Chapter 5

"Just calm *down*, will you? I'm coming as fast as I can!"

"Calm down? Calm down!" As Kate burst out of the trees, she cast a scathing look back over her shoulder and pointed to the bushes alongside the path. "There! Oh, for God's sake, don't *touch* it!"

Tawney stopped near the treeline, her eyes huge. "I don't even want to *see* it! Oh, Denzil, get a stick or something!" She huddled beside Kate, and they watched as Denzil cautiously approached the tangled underbrush.

"Well, there's no cat," he announced tentatively, taking another step closer.

"She probably ran off." Kate shifted nervously, her eyes darting in all directions. "I probably scared her to death when I yelled."

"And there's nothing here," Denzil finished. He slapped his thighs and turned back around. "Well, guess that's that."

"What!" Breaking from Tawney's grasp, Kate came slowly across the grass, eyes narrowed.

"Denzil, if you're just saying that to lure me out here — "

"Ha! Some horror writer *you* are! See for yourself — there's not a thing around here that even *resembles* a — "

"No." Kate shook her head, her chin lifting stubbornly. "No. It was here. I saw it."

"So you saw a glove, big deal. I told you, Pet's the champion thief of all time."

"Denzil, this glove wasn't empty! There was a — *something* — inside it!"

"Mud. Maybe she fished it out of the lake. Or leaves. Maybe she had it buried somewhere—"

"Leaves?" Tawney shivered and stepped back. "Oh, look out, maybe it's hiding under some leaves — "

"Oh, right. It crawled away, and tonight it's gonna scratch on your window." Denzil made his eyes even bigger behind his glasses. "Scratch . . . scratch. . ."

"It's not funny." Kate turned on him. "Pet must have carried it off again. That's the only explanation." She looked at Tawney, who nodded vigorously.

"Wait a minute." Denzil grinned, lowering his head, shaking it slowly from side to side. "Just hold your horses a minute here. Now I see what's going on."

Kate's look was blank. "You do? Then why don't you tell us."

"Ah-ha, pretty sly, you two. *Pretty* sly." His grin spread wider, and he gave a low chuckle. "It's 'cause of that story I told last night, right? Around the fire? The *hand* that should have been a *hook*? Pretty clever, you guys. You *almost* had me convinced."

The girls exchanged bewildered looks, and Kate's cheeks reddened. "Denzil, you are *totally* off base if you think this is some joke. There *was* a glove here, and there *was* something inside it!"

"Yeah, okay." He wagged a finger at them and laughed. "Okay, you two. But I'll get you back! Two can play this game!"

"But there's three of us." Tawney frowned, confused. "And I don't even know what we're playing."

"You wait." Denzil chuckled, heading back onto the path. "I'll definitely get you — and it'll definitely be *good*."

"Denzil" — Kate looked after him beseechingly — "you've *got* to believe me!"

"Hey, *sure* I do!" He doffed his hat and disappeared into the woods. "See you later! And you'd better be ready for anything!"

Kate stared at Tawney, then sighed and climbed up onto the porch. Strange how everything could look so peaceful, so *normal*, when her insides were churning so much. She stared hard at the bushes where she'd last seen Pet . . . let her eyes rove across the clearing and back again. *I couldn't have imagined it. I couldn't have. . . .*

"What did it look like?"

"What?" Kate jumped. She'd almost forgotten Tawney was there.

"You know — that thing you saw. What did it look like?"

"Don't you want to come up here and sit down?"

"No. It might be hiding under your porch."

"Oh, God, Tawney, don't say that!" Kate scooted closer to the door, then stared at the trees and said slowly, "It was brown. Definitely a man's glove. Like a work glove. Real sturdy and thick."

Tawney nodded. "I've seen gloves like that. Pearce wears gloves like that. He wears them all the time when he's working around camp."

Kate considered this, letting out a sigh. "So Pet really *could* have gotten it most anywhere. And what I saw really *wasn't* a hand."

"That's what *I'd* want to believe." Tawney nodded seriously.

Kate regarded her for several minutes. "That'd sure make it easier to stay here tonight."

"I think so, too. Do you want to go swimming later? I know a spot that's kind of secret — we'd have it all to ourselves."

"In *this* weather?" Kate shivered.

"It catches the afternoon sun. It's not so bad."

Once more Kate's eyes circled the clearing, and she tried to sound enthused. "Okay. Sounds like fun."

"Why don't we meet in front of the lodge around four? I don't have to help with dinner tonight, just clean up afterwards."

"I'll be there."

Watching Tawney disappear into the woods, Kate fought back a sudden, overwhelming apprehension. Again she searched the area all around the cabin, not finding a single clue. It *must* have been a mistake, she argued with herself . . . *things like that just don't happen . . . especially to ordinary, boring people like me. . . .*

She let herself in and froze as a new possibility hit her. *Denzil!* Why hadn't she thought of it before? *He* could have easily given Pet the glove, stuffed with God-only-knew-what, and turned her loose on the path . . . he could have hidden in the woods, in hysterics, as she'd made a total fool of herself. Accusing her and Tawney had been a perfect way to avert suspicion — no wonder he'd looked so skeptical when she'd babbled on and on about the thing in the glove! Making a mental note to check out her suspicions with Tawney, Kate stretched out across her bed and opened her notebook.

It was almost like being in class again with Gideon. Scanning her notes, Kate could hear his voice, see the startling color of his eyes, feel the way his gaze had sought her out all through the lecture. Flushing at the memory, Kate sat up and gnawed on the end of her pen. *You've got it bad, girl, so you might as well put it out of your mind right now. He's a teacher, nothing more. To him, you're a dumb student, nothing more. This is an educational experience, and that's as far as it goes.*

"But he did ask me to stay after," Kate mumbled to herself. "He didn't ask anyone else to stay."

That's because everyone else had already gone, stupid.

"I *am* being stupid," Kate grumbled, louder this time. "It's my imagination. It's a curse." She was relieved when four o'clock came — no matter how hard she tried to concentrate on other things, her mind kept going back and forth between Gideon and the thing in Pet's mouth.

Tawney was waiting for her, and the girls set off together past the stables, down a wooded hillside, and out onto a narrow strip of beach. The western sky blazed with late sunlight, sparkling the lake like jewels, and a brisk wind stirred up ruffles across the water. A group of swimmers waved and called, but though Tawney returned their greeting, she led Kate on around a winding curve of rocks and sand.

"Are you sure you know where you're going?" Kate laughed, and Tawney glanced back, motioning her to hurry.

"You'll like it here, I promise. No one ever uses it, 'cause the guests don't know about it."

"Yeah? What about Denzil? Does *he* know about it?"

"Yes, but he doesn't like to swim. See? There it is."

Kate paused and pushed her windblown hair from her face as Tawney scampered the last few feet to the water. The little inlet was nestled between thickly forested banks, and as Kate hurried to catch up, Tawney clambered out onto a huge flat rock and shaded her eyes from a shaft of bright sun.

"See? This rock is really warm, and the water's nice, once you get in. And it's private — that's why I like it."

"It's really beautiful." Kate smiled and climbed up beside her. "Do you come here a lot?"

"As much as I can." Tawney slipped out of her

jeans and T-shirt, and Kate did the same. "Sometimes I don't even swim — I just write my poems. Look — if you get in on this side of the rock, the wind doesn't even touch you."

Kate nodded and lowered herself into the water, surprised at the warmth closing over her shoulders.

"I know!" Tawney hung over the rock, grinning down at her. "Let's skinny-dip!"

"What!" Kate burst out laughing. "We can't do that!"

"Sure we can!"

"No, we can't. What if someone comes along and sees us?"

Tawney's eyes widened, her face going serious. "Oh, but they *won't*. I do it all the time, and nobody's ever seen *me*."

"But, Tawney, how do you know?" Kate shook her head in amusement. "They might have been hiding — just look at all these trees around here."

"No, they wouldn't." Tawney sighed matter-of-factly. "Nobody would look at me. Nobody ever looks at me."

"I don't believe that. You're so pretty."

"No, I'm not. But I think . . ." she cocked her head, considering, "that I have a nice spirit."

Kate laughed, feeling her tension slough off into the soothing water. "Yes, you're right. You *do* have a nice spirit." She bent her head back, the sun soft on her upturned face. "Have you known Denzil very long?"

"We met in the summer. He's taking a year off before he starts college. And I'm just trying to decide what to do with my life . . . I don't want to go to school anymore . . . but I don't think I can get a job anywhere just 'cause I have a nice spirit." She sighed. "What about you?"

"I graduate in the spring. I can't wait." Kate turned her head from side to side, loving the feel of the water upon her cheeks. "Tawney, did it ever occur to you that Denzil might have put that glove there for me to find?"

"Well . . ." The other girl pondered a moment. "I guess he could have. I wasn't with him for a while 'cause I had to take some stuff to one of the cabins."

"I just wondered." Kate tried to force the grisly memory from her mind. "Do you . . . do you know anything about Gideon Drewe?" She hoped her voice was casual, but Tawney didn't seem to think it an odd question.

"Gideon Drewe. Don't you just love his name?" Tawney screwed her face up into the sunlight and squinted her eyes. "Well, we're not personal friends, you know. We've never had a relationship."

Kate smiled. "I sort of guessed that."

"But I hear he's very smart and very talented. And of course you already know how handsome he is." She arched her back and stretched her arms out toward the sun. "I don't think anybody really knows much about the family. They're very private and eccentric." She turned her eyes on Kate, and her expression was solemn. "Gideon has this air about him, don't you think? Like some tragic hero?" She rolled up into a kneeling position and began unhooking the top of her swimsuit.

"Tawney, what are you doing?"

"Taking my clothes off. Oh, I *love* how free I feel this way. Come on, Kate, no one will see us."

Kate watched as Tawney slipped easily into the water, a lithe, shimmering mermaid fishtailing in and out of the light and shadows. As Tawney surfaced a few yards away and shook the hair from her eyes, Kate suddenly laughed and began pulling off her own suit.

"Why not? I'll probably never get to do this again!"

Giggling, they splashed and swam and explored the inlet. Kate had never felt so light and unencumbered, and as they raced the width of the cove and back again, she flung out her arms and floated on her back, savoring the last dying warmth of the sun.

"We'd better get back," Tawney said reluctantly, nodding toward the shadows lengthening along the bank. "I hate to, but it'll get dark pretty soon."

Kate waved her arms lazily, wishing she could float this way forever. "Good idea. I'll get our clothes."

"That's okay. I'm closer."

There was a splash as Tawney pulled herself out of the water. With her mind only half listening, Kate drifted, breathing deeply, and heard the weeds rustling softly along the shore. After several minutes she took one more breath and angled her feet to the solid bottom.

"Tawney, what's the matter? Can't you find — ?"

Her words broke off with a gasp, choking her.

Stumbling backwards, she pushed frantically at

her wet hair, blinking against the unexpected gloom.

The fog was beginning to come in, a gray, silent ghost, hovering over the darkening cove, blurring the trees and shoreline that had seemed so warm and friendly and close before.

But it wasn't the fog that chilled her now, as she stared in disbelief at the murky bank. . . .

It was the tall, silent shadow at the water's edge.

A human shadow.

Black and stark against the gathering night, it raised one arm . . . slowly . . . deliberately . . . in her direction.

And even in her terror, Kate recognized the shape of an axe.

Chapter 6

As instinct took over, Kate swallowed the cry welling up in her throat and eased noiselessly down into the water. Had he seen her? She had no idea how long he'd been standing there as she'd floated so unsuspectingly. She hadn't heard anyone approaching, and now it dawned on her that she hadn't heard a sound from Tawney in quite a while. Had something happened? Surely Kate would have heard a scream — a struggle — *oh, God, Tawney, if you're out there, whatever you do, don't come back this way. . . .*

Slipping smoothly underwater, Kate glided over to the rock and surfaced slowly, praying she hadn't given away her whereabouts. Pressing against the stone, she peered toward the bank.

The shadow was gone.

With a sharp intake of breath, Kate froze. The wind whispered through the trees, rustling the branches all around her. The wind . . . *or footsteps*? Her heart thudded sickeningly in her chest, and she wrapped her arms around herself to keep from shaking. From somewhere along the bank, a twig snapped. . . .

And something slipped into the water.

Panic-stricken, Kate ducked behind the rock, her fingers working frantically for a place to hold on. The water was growing colder, twilight noises growing louder. *He could be anywhere . . . on the bank beside me . . . behind me . . . in the water . . . oh, God, Tawney, where are you?*

"Kate!"

Forgetting caution, Kate paddled out into the water and saw Tawney huddled on the bank where the shadow had been only moments before. "Hurry! Throw me my clothes!"

"But that's just it." Tawney sounded bewildered. "I can't find them!"

"What!"

"I can't find our clothes! I've looked and looked and they're not anywhere! And now it's getting dark and I forgot to bring a flashlight!"

Kate stared at the girl's outline through the thickening fog, at the trees around her with their limbs outstretched. One branch lifted on a breath of wind, a shockingly human movement.

"I don't know what to do," Tawney was saying. "We can't go back to camp without our clothes and — "

"Tawney, did you hear anything while you were looking? Did you see anything? Anybody?" Kate was close to shore now, close enough to see Tawney shake her head.

"No. Why?"

Kate's eyes slowly swept the embankment, coming to rest uneasily on that one oddly shaped tree. *I could have imagined it . . . I must have imagined it. . . .* "I — "

She broke off abruptly as something crashed through the woods behind Tawney. With a scream, Tawney landed in the water beside her, and they held onto each other as a shadow burst out through the trees.

"Well, hey there, strangers. I figured I'd find you here."

"Denzil!" Kate burst out angrily and lowered herself deeper into the lake.

"Yep, you're lookin' at him. And Tawney, you're late for work — just in case you hadn't noticed."

"I *am*?" Tawney's eyes grew wide and confused. "I thought I cleaned up tonight — did I read the schedule wrong *again*?"

Denzil sighed and nodded. "Come on, you two, you're lookin' to catch pneumonia."

"No," Tawney said bluntly, "we're looking for our clothes. Oh, Denzil, we can't find our clothes *anywhere*!"

"Your clothes?" Denzil looked surprised, his eyes automatically scanning the ground around his feet. "Where'd you leave them?"

"There." Tawney pointed. "We threw them on the bank right there."

"Well, just come on back now — we can look for them tomorrow when it's light."

"No," Tawney protested, "I mean, we don't have

anything! Our swimsuits or *anything*! We took *everything* off!"

"Your clothes," Denzil muttered again. "Everything." He scratched his chin, his hat slipping back from his forehead. "Hmmm . . . this *is* an interesting predicament."

"It's not funny." Kate glared at him. "This is serious!"

"Yes . . . oh, yes, it is." From the sound of his voice, Kate could tell he was struggling to keep a straight face. "*Verrry* serious."

"Denzil!"

"Okay," he chuckled, moving back up the incline, "don't get panicky. I'll have a look around."

Kate was beginning to feel like one giant goosebump. When Denzil finally reappeared, she looked hopefully at something dangling from his hands.

"Did you find them?" Tawney's voice was pleading. "I just *can't* go back to camp without my clothes. I'd rather *die* than — "

"I think this is them," Denzil said, but there was something odd about the way he said it, something that made new goosebumps prickle along Kate's arms. "At least," Denzil added, "what's left of them."

Squatting down at the water's edge, he held up a lump of material and shook it out. Kate felt herself going stiff, her mind reeling as Tawney made a funny sound in her throat.

What had once been Kate's swimsuit and T-shirt now hung in shreds, the fabric ripped and stained with something dark. . . .

"This is it," Denzil said quietly. "This is all I found."

Kate felt numb all over. She stared at the tatters, her voice hoarse. "Those . . . are mine. . . ."

"Oh, isn't that just our luck," Tawney sighed, exasperated. "Some bear hauled off our clothes and *ate* them!"

"There aren't any bears around here, Tawney," Denzil said.

"Well, *what* then?" Tawney sounded totally bewildered. "What — ?"

"An axe," Kate mumbled, and then louder, "an axe. Someone with an axe."

"An axe?" Now Denzil looked confused. "Who would go around chopping up clothes? These things look like they were slashed. Like with a knife or something." He looked up and suddenly said, "Whoa — hold on a minute — "

As the girls stared, he disappeared into the shadows, emerging a moment later with a small bundle.

"Look what I just found — all wadded up on that branch like a bird's nest. Tawney, are these yours?"

As he shook the clothes loose, Tawney clapped her hands, nearly coming out of the water.

"Oh, Denzil, you found them! And they're not all cut up! You're a hero! But what are we going to do about Kate?"

"What *are* we gonna do about Kate?" Denzil echoed.

"I don't know," Tawney shook her head. "What?"

"I'd give her my jacket," Denzil considered, "but I don't think it'd cover enough."

"Then give her your shirt," Tawney ordered him. "It's got a long tail, and it's almost dark now anyway — it'll be fine till she gets to her cabin."

Denzil was holding up Kate's mutilated things again, his expression serious. "Maybe it *was* some kind of animal. Maybe Pet got ahold of it. Maybe she hid the rest somewhere. . . ."

Kate stared at him a minute, and then a slow, seething anger began to creep over her.

"You!"

"Me what?"

"*You* did this! Oh, Denzil, I can't believe you'd stoop so *low*! The clothes — the axe — "

"Whoa, *whoa*!" Denzil jumped up. "What are you *talking* about?"

"This!" Kate exploded. It was all she could do to keep from flying out of the water and going for his throat. "You *planned* this, didn't you? To get us back for that *stupid* glove — you really *do* think we tried to play a joke on you!"

"You think *I* did this?" Denzil's voice went high with astonishment. "Sliced up your clothes? And *what's* all this stuff about an axe — ?"

"The man I saw on the bank," Kate babbled. "While Tawney was looking for our things — he came out of the trees and he had an axe — "

Tawney's scream cut her off, and both she and Denzil jumped.

"Tawney, what is it?"

"Oh! I'm just so *scared*! That a crazy person was here and I didn't even *know*! I didn't even have my *clothes*!"

"There's no crazy person! For crying out loud," Denzil muttered, shrugging out of his jacket. "This is all I need — hysterical women and — "

"I am *not* hysterical." Kate pointed toward the trees behind him. "He slipped right out of there with his axe."

"It was probably Pearce." Denzil pulled off his shirt and threw it on the ground. "Pearce! He's always chopping wood around here. What were you doing, anyway?"

"I was . . ." Kate felt her cheeks burn, "floating."

"Floating. Right." Denzil sounded smug. "I'm sure he had quite a view."

"I'm cold," Tawney reminded him. "Can we get out now?"

"I'll see you back at camp."

"No, you have to wait for us, we don't have a flashlight."

"Terrific."

They could still hear him grumbling as he stepped back into the trees. Cautiously they went toward the bank, hesitating at the water's edge.

"Don't you dare look!" Kate shouted.

"Don't flatter yourself!"

The girls dressed in record time, and with Denzil in the lead, made their way back to camp. Denzil's shirt barely covered the tops of Kate's thighs, and though she kept trying to pull it down, she was painfully aware of how little it concealed. As they reached the path to her cabin, Denzil suddenly turned and looked at her.

"You . . . uh . . . gonna be okay?"

"Fine. I'll be fine."

He nodded slowly . . . turned to go . . . turned back around.

"Hey . . . whatever you think . . . I've been in the kitchen all day. You can ask around."

Kate nodded back reluctantly. "Well . . . I'll see you tomorrow."

"You turning in already? Movies in the lodge later."

"I'll see. I'm pretty tired, though."

"Don't you even wanna eat? It's still early."

She shrugged, pulling at her shirt.

"Well, at least take my flashlight. I can get another one."

"Thanks."

"You're welcome. Nice legs."

Kate grabbed the flashlight and hurried away. As her cabin came into view, she slowed down and reached automatically for her keys.

The pocket of Denzil's shirt gaped open. Empty.

"Oh, no, I can't believe this," Kate groaned. She was shivering now, with frustration as well as with cold, and she banged on the door in hopes that Miss Bunceton might be inside. When nobody answered she stepped back off the porch, her heart sinking. *They're probably back there by the lake . . . somewhere in the grass . . . they fell out of my clothes. . . .*

If someone didn't take them.

Kate froze, her mind racing. Tawney's clothes hadn't been destroyed, only hers. And Tawney hadn't seen the man beside the lake, only she had.

And the menacing shadow had only come after Tawney was gone. . . .

"It was Denzil," Kate muttered. It *had* to have been him, watching them swim, waiting for his chance to get even. She wasn't going to let another stupid practical joke send her into a tailspin — she'd just find Tawney and go back to search for her keys.

As she reached the road, Kate suddenly realized how impossible her mission was going to be. She had no idea where Tawney was, and she certainly couldn't go looking for her dressed like this. The same went for Miss Bunceton — and Kate refused to sit on the cabin steps in the cold waiting for someone to show up.

"Damn!" Trying to keep close to the shadows, Kate retraced her earlier trek to the lake, trying to remember where Tawney had turned off to the inlet. Here? She paused, confused, playing the flashlight across the leaves. It didn't look right — but everything seemed different at night . . . alone. . . .

Shaking off her nervousness, Kate continued on, finally spotting a path that looked familiar. She took a deep breath and plunged into the woods.

The darkness was deceiving. As Kate went deeper and deeper into it, she had no idea how far she'd come or how long she'd been walking. Once she finally admitted to herself that she was on the wrong trail, she tried to backtrack and lost all sense of direction, her growing fear causing her to follow any footpath she came across. Branches clawed at her face and hair, ripping Denzil's shirt. She didn't know if the dampness on her cheeks was blood or fog or frightened tears, and she began to run.

"Help!" she called, but she wasn't sure if the cry was real or only in her mind. "Somebody — I'm lost — help me!"

Without warning she stumbled out into a wide, open space and sprawled face down on the wet ground.

Silence. As she slowly lifted her head, the silence was deep and terrifying. Blinking through the heavy gray mist, she saw a pale glow in the distance. And then, as her eyes grew more accustomed to the night, she saw something else that made her raise up and stare.

It was a gate. A tall, iron gate looming up against the dark. With the soft light beyond it, Kate could see its perfect silhouette, the sharp spikes along the top. Locating her fallen flashlight, she shone it through the bars.

There was a house behind the fence, huge and black and grotesque, like some awful nightmare rendered in charcoal across the sky.

The light was coming from one upstairs window.

Kate reached her other hand forward to push herself up. . . .

And touched someone's bare foot.

Shrieking, she jumped up, the flashlight beam slicing crazily through the gloom.

"Scream . . . scream . . ." a voice sang softly. "Trapped in a dream. . . ."

It was an eerie voice . . . hoarse and whispery . . . as if every word were painful, and as Kate fumbled her light and aimed it full force onto the stranger's face, she gasped at what she saw.

The thing standing before her was dressed all in black, long black skirts trailing limply in the grass, a long black veil swathing the body . . . the head . . . the hidden eyes. . . .

"My God," Kate mumbled, "who are you?"

"I'm Rowena." The visage swayed a little, blending itself into the cover of trees and shadows and fathomless night. "And you're Kate. Kate . . . Kate . . . doomed to your fate."

Chapter 7

Kate peered hard into the darkness. The phantom swayed calmly . . . teasingly . . . just beyond reach of the flashlight.

"How do you know me?" Kate murmured. "How do you know my name?"

The veil fluttered softly. Somehow Kate knew that she was being carefully scrutinized.

"He talks about you . . . he thinks you're beautiful. . . ."

"Who?" Slowly Kate backed away, her voice quivering. "I don't know what you're talking about. I took the wrong path — "

"Death. . . ." The voice dropped even more, black-gloved hands disappearing into the black folds of material. "Don't you feel it? We're all dead here . . . all . . . very . . . dead." The head raised as Kate took a clumsy step sideways. "Come inside. Come . . . don't be afraid."

"No . . . really . . . I need to get back — "

"I'll show you secrets if you stay." The gravelly voice hinted of a smile. "You'll never know if you run away. Come . . . come inside . . ."

Kate looked again at the bleak house beyond the fence, at the window with its one feeble light. "No, I have to go. I didn't know anyone lived back here."

Was that a laugh? That horrible, guttural sound so deep in the throat? The long skirts whispered, and again Kate moved back.

"No one does," the voice replied. "The house is empty."

"Do you . . . do you live here alone?"

The shadow hesitated . . . shook its head. One arm lifted . . . beckoned toward Kate. "Come with me . . . come and see. . . ."

"No — "

"Come and see . . . come with me — "

As the voice kept repeating its macabre little chant, the figure advanced on Kate, forcing her back into the trees. In the pale light, through the shifting fog, Rowena seemed to hover above the ground, her fingers fluttering like tiny black moths.

"Pretty Kate," she whispered, "just like he said. . . ."

"Who said?" Kate's voice shook. "Please . . . I don't know — "

"You mustn't tell. You mustn't tell about me."

The figure came closer. Kate's fear choked her, and she backed against the trunk of a tree. "No . . . I mean, no, not if you don't want me to — "

"Someone told . . . now he's cold. . . ."

"I won't — "

"I'll know if you do. I'll find out."

"Yes. Yes — I promise."

The hand reached out for her . . . inches from her face. . . .

"I won't tell!" Kate cried. "I didn't mean to come! I'm sorry — "

"Yes," and that strange thick laugh came again. "You will be."

Kate whirled and plunged into the woods — trees, shadows, darkness, all rushing by in a blur. She didn't know where she was running, but as she crashed out onto the beach at last, she didn't stop until she saw her cabin up ahead and the two shadowy figures banging on her door.

"Kate! Are you in there? Are you okay?" Denzil's voice sounded worried, and he started pounding again.

"I don't think she's in there," Tawney said. "Oh, I hope the swimsuit thing didn't get her — "

"The swimsuit thing? What — ?"

"Here I am!" Kate called, and forced herself to walk, smoothing her hair with trembling fingers. *I can't tell them where I've been . . . I promised Rowena . . . she said I'd be sorry. . . .*

"Kate!" Denzil was at her side in an instant, his face struggling between anger and relief. "Where *were* you? We were about to call out the posse!" He played his flashlight over Kate's bare legs and grinned as she tried to pull the shirt down.

"I thought you'd been kidnapped!" Tawney exclaimed. "I thought someone got you with an axe! I thought — "

"My keys," Kate said quickly. "They must have fallen out of my T-shirt when we got undressed to go swimming. I was . . . checking along the road."

"Funny." Denzil stared at her. "We didn't see you on our way."

"Oh, Kate." Tawney gave her a sympathetic hug. "I bet you lost them in the weeds back there. You'll never find them now." She stopped, considering. "Or else the axeman took them."

"Thanks, Tawney." Denzil gave an exaggerated smile. "I'm sure she feels *real* good now."

"Denzil," Kate said angrily, "if you — "

"I don't wanna hear it. I *don't* have your keys. I *don't* have an axe, and I *didn't* shred your clothes. Come on." He slid his arm around Kate's other shoulder, hurrying the girls along. "You're gonna catch pneumonia if you don't get some dry clothes. We can worry about the keys later."

"You're about my size," Tawney piped up. "You can wear something of mine. And you can stay with me tonight, too, if you can't get into your cabin."

"Oh, I'm sure Miss Bunceton will be back later," Kate assured her. "I'd just feel better if I had my own key."

"Pearce should have one." Denzil shrugged. "He has keys to all the buildings."

Just the thought of that made Kate uneasy, and she tried to put it out of her mind.

It only took a few minutes to change into some of Tawney's clothes, but Kate's chilled feeling remained. As she and Denzil and Tawney approached the lodge, she saw Pearce standing on the porch watching them, his lean body pressed back against one of the wooden columns. Pretending she hadn't noticed him, she went inside, glad for the cheery log fire and the people milling around exchanging the day's experiences. She and Tawney found a couch near the hearth, and Denzil joined them a moment later, bringing cups of spiced cider.

"I don't see Miss Bunceton." Kate scanned the crowded room.

"I heard some people talking." Denzil jerked his chin toward one noisy group. "There's a discussion going on over in the dining hall. Romantic classics."

"Then that's where she'll be. She'd never pass that up."

"Hey, look," Denzil said, deadpan. "There's Igor."

Kate followed the point of his finger and saw Pearce leaning silently in the opposite corner. "Don't you think it's creepy the way he's always watching everybody?" she whispered.

"He undresses me with his eyes," Tawney said, her own eyes going bigger. "It's not a very nice feeling."

Denzil gave her a skeptical look. "More like he's undressing your mind. You have nothing to worry about."

"Oh," Tawney breathed, "good. That's a relief."

"Denzil!" Kate scolded.

"Hey, it's okay," he said innocently. "How can I hurt her feelings if she doesn't even get the joke?"

Tawney stared at him. "What joke?"

Kate glanced again toward the far corner. Pearce drew back against the wall and slid out a side doorway.

"Hey, you sure you're okay?" Denzil touched Kate's arm, frowning as she jumped.

"Yes . . . I . . . just have a lot on my mind." Forcing a smile, Kate stood up, half expecting Pearce to reappear without warning in the shadows beside the fire. She didn't see Gideon anywhere. "I'm going to try and find Miss Bunceton."

"Okay. See you later, pardner." Denzil touched his hat.

"And come stay with me if you need a place," Tawney reminded her. "I have to go back to work now, but I'll be in cabin three, over where the employees stay. Cabin three, next to Denzil."

"And if she's asleep, you can stay with me." Denzil grinned. "Cabin four. Next to Tawney."

"I'll keep that in mind," Kate promised.

Quiet descended as she walked quickly to the dining hall. Darting a look back over her shoulder, she tried to control the fear and confusion in her mind. She could still see Rowena . . . could still feel the panic of that ghostly encounter . . . *like something in a nightmare, someone all dressed up for a funeral, someone dead. . . .* She could still hear that gravelly voice . . . the strange singsong rhymes . . . *"I'll show you secrets if you stay . . . you'll never know if you run away. . . ."*

Kate walked faster, heart pounding. *"He talks about you . . . he thinks you're beautiful. . . ."*

"Kate . . . Kate . . . doomed to your fate."

She began to run, eyes straight on the road and away from the shifting shadows, but the dining hall was deserted when she got there. Hoping Miss

Bunceton might be at the cabin by now, Kate turned back and spied a lone shadow sitting on some steps across the road. There was the scratch of a match, a hiss of flame, and an eerie image of Pearce's face only an instant before the flame went out. Kate froze, her eyes glued in sudden, clutching fear upon the darkness. Another match flared . . . flickered . . . fell into the dirt and went out.

"Pearce?" she called weakly.

No answer.

Taking a deep breath, she forced herself to cross the road and stopped a safe distance away from him.

"Pearce," she said again, trying to control the trembling in her voice. "Denzil said I should talk to you. I lost the key to my cabin, and he said you might have an extra one."

Even in the pale light from the window, Pearce seemed more shadow than human. She could feel him watching her, and in spite of her dry clothes, she felt chilled all over again.

"I might," he said, after endless minutes. "I'll have to check."

"I'd really appreciate it if you would." Her voice sounded thin, and she watched as his hand lifted toward his face.

Another match flared . . . sputtered . . . died.

"Cabin thirteen. Isn't it?"

A new trembling threatened her voice, but she choked it back. "Yes." And even though she couldn't see him clearly, she thought he might have nodded.

"I'll see what I can do."

"Thanks. Well . . . good night."

All she wanted to do was get away from him. She started down the road when his voice stopped her.

"I hear you're quite the writer. Quite the teacher's pet."

"I . . . I don't know what you mean."

"No? Then maybe you're in for a surprise. And maybe it won't be a nice one."

Kate heard her voice lashing out, braver than she felt. "I don't know what you're talking about. But nothing that pertains to me is *any* of your business."

The match hissed again. She saw his black, black eyes flickering.

"You're right. How inconsiderate of me."

Shaken, Kate willed her feet to move her forward.

"You should be more careful," Pearce said. "Anyone could find your key. Anyone could get into your cabin."

Kate whirled to face him. "I have a roommate. I'm not alone."

"A roommate?" And he sounded like he was smiling . . . a dark, strange smile as if she'd said something peculiarly funny. "If someone wanted to get you," Pearce said slowly, and another match went out, "a roommate wouldn't stop them. They'd just get you. Wouldn't they."

Chapter 8

"Kate, dear, is something wrong?" Miss Bunceton gulped down a forkful of scrambled eggs and looked worriedly at the girl beside her. "You're so pale this morning. Don't tell me you're still upset about that wretched key — it could happen to anyone. Let's just hide it someplace outside the cabin — "

"No," Kate said quickly, "don't hide it." Her brain felt like wet sand. All night she'd dreamed about Rowena, waking up in a cold sweat. *How does she know me?*

"Kate?"

"I'll just find you if I need to get in," Kate mumbled. "It's not a big deal." *Someone might have my key . . . someone who's been talking about me to Rowena. . . .*

"Well, please don't fret. You're here to *enjoy* yourself, for goodness' sake. Don't let trivialities upset you so."

Kate nodded and pretended to eat her breakfast, looking up again as Denzil hissed at her from the doorway.

"Excuse me," Kate mumbled, and before Miss Bunceton could reply, she hurried into the kitchen.

"You can't fool me," Denzil chided. "You weren't eating. You were hiding everything under your toast — it's the oldest trick in the book."

"I helped cook this morning," Tawney said, spatula in hand. "People always hide things under their toast when I help cook."

"No, it was fine, really. I'm just not hungry." Kate debated whether or not to tell them about her strange confrontation with Pearce last night but decided against it. Pearce was just being his usual weird self, and she was just being paranoid. There hadn't been anyone at the inlet with an axe, and some animal had simply dragged off her clothes and she'd only imagined that hand . . . *but the house and Rowena were real . . . weren't they?*

"Are you listening?" Denzil gave her a shake, and Kate stared at him stupidly.

"I'm sorry. What?"

"I said I have to go into the village this morning for supplies. Wanna tag along?"

"I'm going, too," Tawney said. "It's a pretty ride. And we can get lunch there 'cause Denzil and I don't have kitchen duty."

Kate glanced at her watch. "What time are you going?"

"Couple hours?" Denzil said. "Soon as we finish up here."

"Do you have a class, Kate?" Tawney fanned herself with a dishrag and sidestepped a girl bustling out with sausages.

"I have to meet with Gideon. He's critiquing my story."

"Oh, isn't that so romantic." Tawney sighed.

"Yeah, aren't you lucky." Denzil shook his head and slammed the pantry door. "What is this — Gideon week? Aren't you going to any *other* classes while you're here?"

"I happen to *like* horror," Kate said. "I have lots to learn."

"Yeah, he looks like the type you could learn a lot from, all right."

"Well, why would you *want* to take any other classes if you can have Gideon?" Tawney looked perplexed.

"I don't *have* Gideon." Kate turned to her. "He's just — "

"Shame on you." Denzil fixed her with a deadpan stare. "Falling in love while poor William's still not accounted for."

"Ooh." Tawney shivered before Kate could answer. "I think it's scary the way he's just disappeared this long. I heard some of the instructors talking out by the lodge this morning. . . ." She paused dramatically, making sure she had their attention. "And they said maybe something really *happened* to him!"

"Something *did* happen to him." Denzil snorted. "He got loaded and forgot where he was supposed to be."

"Do you think so?" Tawney looked worried. "Do you think he's really lost?"

"Sure he is," Denzil said solemnly. "Why . . . he

could be anywhere." He went over to a pot on the stove and cautiously lifted off the lid. "William? William, are you in there?"

"I'm going," Kate announced. "Where do you want to meet?"

"Out front. Two hours." Denzil looked immensely pleased with himself. "So is this a *private* meeting? Just a one-on-one critique? Just a cozy little twosome kind of talk?"

"Business," Kate reminded him. "Strictly business."

Gideon was already there when she reached the cabin. He was sitting at one of the tables, his head bent over a stack of papers, Pet sprawled at his feet. At the sound of Kate's footsteps, he looked up and stopped her in the doorway with his smile.

"Kate. I was afraid you'd back out on me."

"I'm tough." Kate grinned. "I can take it."

"Then you're going to be awfully disappointed if you've prepared yourself for negatives. Your work is exceptionally good."

Kate couldn't keep from blushing. She busied herself taking off her jacket and jumped nervously as Gideon patted a chair.

"Sit down. We'll go over your manuscript page by page."

Kate nodded, then hesitated, biting her lip. "Gideon?"

"Yes."

"I heard . . . I mean . . . I hope you don't think I'm being nosy or anything, but have you heard anything about William?"

For a moment Gideon said nothing, his head bowed once again over his work. One hand lay outstretched beside the papers, and as she watched, his fingers curled, one by one, into a fist.

"No, I haven't," he said quietly. "But thank you."

When he didn't speak again, Kate sat down, her voice anxious.

"If you're worried about the class, don't be. Everyone's really glad you took it over. Just the fact that you were nice enough to show up was way more than anyone — "

"It's all right, Kate. I know you're trying to help." He looked up then, catching her in the deep violet glow of his eyes. "William and I aren't close. In fact," he looked away, "I don't much care for him at all."

Kate didn't know what to say. Feeling foolish for having intruded, she fidgeted in her chair and waited for him to go on.

"To be truthful, I'm not sure William has any *real* friends," Gideon said offhandedly. "Just leeches and hangers-on that tell him what he wants to hear."

"Oh. I thought maybe he was a recluse. Like a lot of writers are."

"He's an alcoholic and a tyrant. He lives on dreams that will never come true because he won't try."

"But . . . he did write that one book — "

"He didn't," Gideon said, facing her again. "It was *my* novel that was published. My novel under his name."

Kate's mouth dropped open. "But . . . why? I don't understand."

"It was part of an agreement," Gideon said, shuffling his papers, tapping them edgewise on the table. "Anyway, it doesn't matter, and it's certainly nothing for you to concern yourself with. I shouldn't have said anything. I'd rather you just forget this whole unpleasant conversation about William." It was said so dispassionately that Kate stared at him. "We're here to talk about *your* story now and *your* talent. You *are* very talented, Kate. I think that with a little luck, you'll have a brilliant future ahead if you stick with your writing. You show perceptions far beyond your years."

"Why . . . I — " Kate stammered, surprised. "It's just a story, just a class assignment — "

"It has depth. Feeling. Trust me, Kate." Gideon smiled. "It's really very good."

Kate looked down, her hands twisting in her lap. "Well . . . thank you."

"You're blushing." Gideon sounded amused. "And there's no reason to. Although you're very pretty when you do."

Kate stared hard at the table, concentrated on the grain of the wood, the pencil marks, the ink stains.

"I *am* embarrassing you. I'm sorry. I'll get on with your story, and then you can take your eyes off that table."

Relieved, Kate forgot her self-consciousness and concentrated on Gideon's critique. It was good to get his perspective on her work, constructive criticism from someone other than Miss Bunceton or her creative writing class. She'd always hoped, deep down, that she was good — but now, listening to Gideon, she believed she *could* be a writer, that her dream *could* come true. As he turned the last page, her mind soared with promise, and her heart felt ready to burst.

"The end," Gideon said softly. "But, of course, it's only the beginning for you."

"Do you really think I'm good? That I *could* be good?" She knew she sounded silly and overeager, but she couldn't hold back her excitement.

"You *are* good. Today. Here and now. And with dedication, you'll only get better."

Kate leaned back in her chair, eyes glowing. There was something so magical about Gideon — the spell he wove with his soft voice and his calm, gentle eyes that made time seem to stop and the world seem right again.

"I feel like walking," Gideon said, and stood up, stretching. "It's a beautiful morning. Walk with me, Kate."

"Well. . . ." She glanced at her watch. Denzil had said two hours, yet she didn't feel like leaving yet . . . or giving up the wonderful feeling she had inside.

"I have to be back soon," she admitted reluctantly. "I'm meeting some friends."

"That's no problem. This won't take long."

"Where are we going?"

"The woods are beautiful this time of morning." He winked. "I know trails you wouldn't even dream of."

A sudden flash went through her mind: the gloomy house beyond the fence, the whispering figure in black. She'd been trying so hard not to think about it, but now she shivered as he took her arm and led her away from the cabin.

"Cold?" Gideon glanced down, yet even as Kate shook her head, he slipped one arm around her shoulders and smiled. "It never gets very warm under all these trees — the sun just can't get through. I suppose that's one of the reasons I love it so much. It's so dark . . . so mysterious." He glanced down at her again, his expression thoughtful. "Anything could happen in here. Anything. And no one would ever know."

Kate felt a chill go up her spine and told herself it was only the weather. "It sounds like you're plotting a story," she laughed.

"Does it?" Gideon looked amused. "Well, I'm more than glad to share. Perhaps you can store this lovely place away in your memory and use it someday. Perhaps I'll be in there, as well." For a moment his eyes looked deeply into hers, then he shook his head. "How presumptuous of me. I apologize."

"You don't have to." Kate looked away, embarrassed. "How did you ever decide to be a writer?"

"Sometimes I think I was ill-fated," Gideon chuckled. "We were a very creative family. My parents were in the theater, and we used to write and act out plays at home." He guided her around a fallen log, smiling at the memory. "William had the ego, the self-centeredness. He loved to show off. Pearce — oh, yes, we go way back — he was superb at imitation . . . he could look and sound like anyone and anything. His parents worked for mine — his father was our caretaker and his mother was our cook — but he was like a brother to me. More a brother to me than William ever was. . . ." His voice faded, some long-ago emotion softening it even more. "How grand we were then. How very ignorant of our mortality." He plucked a dead leaf, crunching it between his fingers. "My parents died in an accident. Pearce's parents had gone to pick them up from the airport, and it was raining. They came to a railroad crossing guard that wasn't working. All four of them were killed instantly."

Kate closed her eyes against his pain, against the brutal story that had no place here in this safe, peaceful world.

"William, my steady older brother, took to drinking instead of responsibilities, and the family nest egg got frittered away bit by bit to pay off his debts. Now we have the camp, which we rent out, and the summer home, where William holds court. I teach classes at a private school, several towns north of here — and then, of course, there's my writing, which hardly allows us to live like kings."

"And your summer home — " Kate stopped, biting her lip. Again Rowena's warning came back to her, and she thought carefully before adding, "Is it . . . very near here?"

Was it her imagination or did Gideon's glance

seem unusually sharp? His arm slid from her shoulder and he held back a low branch for her to pass under.

"It's back in the woods away from everything. Guests would *not* be welcome, I'm afraid. William's very . . . unpredictable."

Kate waited for him to catch up. "What about Pearce?"

"He takes care of the camp. The rest of the time he does labor . . . odd jobs down in the village and towns nearby. He's an excellent craftsman . . . excellent with his hands. This was all woodland when we were children — Pearce's father cleared it all out, and he and Pearce built most of the cabins themselves. Pearce took over after he died."

"So that's where you stay when you're here?" Kate tried to sound casual. "In your summerhouse, I mean? You and Pearce?"

Gideon cast her a curious glance. "Pearce has his own cabin in the woods. But yes, we both stay there if we need to."

Then it must be the same house.

"Just the two of you? No one else?"

"Well . . . William, of course." Gideon shrugged. "And his strange assortment of women friends from time to time."

"Oh?"

"An odd bunch, if ever there was one. Very much into the macabre." Gideon shook his head. "That's why Pearce stays clear of the place for the most part. I believe he refers to them as Horror Groupies. I despise them being there."

Of course . . . then that explains it . . . Rowena must be one of William's weird friends. . . . Catching Gideon's eye upon her, Kate hurriedly changed the subject. "I'm always so interested in big families. I don't have brothers or sisters."

"I'd hardly call us a family."

Kate studied the leaf-deep path at her feet. "Oh, but your life would be so interesting to so many people. Why don't you write a book about it?"

"I can't, can I?" Gideon smiled mysteriously. "Since I don't know yet how it ends." As Kate gave him a curious glance, he added, "You're the storyteller, Kate. Tell me how it ends."

"Well" — she laughed self-consciously, not sure what he meant — "I'm not that good at plotting. I sort of put things down when they come into my mind."

"Ah. An instinctive writer. I see." Gideon nodded, more to himself than to her. "You're very good with your instincts. And with fear." His eyes lowered, settling on her face. "You're very good with fear."

"Fear?" Kate gave a laugh, shrugging her shoulders. "Everyone should be able to write about fear, shouldn't they? Everyone's afraid of something."

"Yes, it's sad, isn't it," Gideon said quietly. "Fear is such a stealthy thing . . . it can consume you slowly." He cast her a sidelong glance. "And you, Kate . . . what are *you* afraid of?"

"Oh, I don't know." She walked faster, suddenly wishing he'd change the subject. "I kind of like being scared."

"And nothing *really* frightens you?"

"Oh, well, sure." She laughed nervously. "Being trapped. Bad surprises. Hopeless situations, things like — "

Stopping suddenly, she spun around, searching the deep, silent woods.

"Did you hear something?"

Gideon's expression was startled. "No. What did you hear?"

"It sounded like footsteps. Like someone following us."

"No one could be following us, Kate. None of the guests even know about this path — it's not on the map."

"But I heard *something* . . . I know I did."

"The wind, most likely." Gideon's voice was casual, but as Kate looked up at him, a muscle moved in his cheek. He glanced away, his eyes quickly sweeping their surroundings. "Only the wind. Come on."

Without warning his hand closed around hers, and a strange thrill went through her fingertips, driving all fearful thoughts from her mind. His touch was so strong, yet so gentle, and from time to time she stole a look at his handsome profile when she was sure he wasn't looking. *I can't believe I'm here . . . I can't believe this is really happening. . . .*

"Kate?"

"Yes?" She flushed, realizing she'd missed something.

"You haven't heard a word I've said. Are you

still worrying about that noise you thought you heard?" His hands lifted to her shoulders and he turned her to face him, looking down with a teasing smile. "Is all this talk about fear upsetting you?"

She tried to look away but couldn't. "No. Of course not — I'm not afraid — "

His fingers reached gently, caressing her hair, her cheek. His smile faded, going pensive as he stared at her. "At least, not of me, I hope. You're *not* afraid of me, are you, Kate?"

She opened her mouth to answer . . . felt his lips upon hers, taking her breath away . . . and as Gideon's mouth moved to her chin . . . to her throat . . . she gasped and felt his arms around her, urging her nearer.

"Gideon," she mumbled, but no sound came out, and warmth and weakness rushed over her as he lifted his head at last and held her close.

It seemed forever that they stood there. Around them the forest stirred with secret rustlings. As Gideon finally loosened his hold and stepped away, Kate smoothed her blouse with shaky fingers.

"Come on," Gideon said. "I thought you had to meet someone."

"Yes," Kate murmured, "yes, I should get back. . . ."

He didn't take her hand this time. He walked ahead, his face lowered, and occasionally cast a look back to make sure she was following. A hundred emotions raged through Kate as she stared at the lines of his back . . . at his sure, easy walk. She could still feel the warmth of his lips upon hers, and in sudden embarrassment she tripped over an exposed tree root and went sprawling onto the trail.

"Kate, are you all right?"

Gideon was beside her in an instant, his arms beneath her, pulling her up. As Kate struggled to get her footing, something in the underbrush caught her eye and she froze, a surge of anger bringing her wildly to her feet.

"*Denzil!* I should have known!"

Thrown off balance by her unexpected rage, Gideon grabbed for a tree and stared at Kate as though she'd lost her mind.

"Kate — in heaven's name — what — ?"

"*He's* been here!" Kate sputtered. "I *told* you I heard something — and now he's playing that *stupid* joke again — "

"What *joke*? What are you talking about?"

"That stupid *glove*!" To Gideon's dismay, Kate made a dive into the weeds and came up with something in her hand. "See this?" She waved it under his nose, seething. "Denzil must have done it. He *had* to have done it!"

Gideon watched as she hurled the thing onto the ground. "What stupid glove? And who is Denzil?"

"Denzil Doyle," Kate muttered. "Oh, just *wait* till I get him! He works in the kitchen. He's in your class with me."

"Doyle . . . Doyle. . . ." Gideon nodded. "Yes, of course, I just couldn't place the name with the face for a moment, but of course I know who he is."

Kate took a deep breath. "You do?"

"I had him in a summer class." Gideon cast her

a rueful look. "I'm rather afraid he didn't much like me."

"*You* had him for a class?"

"Yes, at a conference here, as a matter of fact. I remember it distinctly — I didn't think he was very good. Oh, don't get me wrong, his ideas were passing, but the execution. . . ." Gideon shook his head. "To be perfectly honest, I'm very surprised to see him in a class of mine again. We had some heated discussions last time around. He was very opinionated."

"And he has a sick sense of humor." Kate glowered down at the thing in the dirt. "But he's not very clever — I mean, this *proves* he planted that other glove by my cabin."

"Please." Gideon held up his hands, approaching her cautiously. "Will you *please* tell me what you're talking about?"

"This glove." Kate picked it up by one limp finger. "Yesterday by my cabin, Pet had a glove just like this, only it — well. . . ." Somehow, repeating it now in front of Gideon made it sound all the more ridiculous. "When I took it from her, it had . . . I mean, it felt like it had a — Gideon, what's wrong?"

In alarm, Kate saw the color slowly drain from Gideon's face, his eyes fixed wide upon the glove in her hand.

"Gideon?"

"Let me see that," he murmured, and as Kate held it out to him, she could see his fingers trembling ever so slightly.

"Gideon, what is it?" Her voice rose anxiously as

he turned the glove over and over in his hand, running one thumb over the thick seams . . . the dark stains. . . .

"See?" Cautiously she touched one of them, a dark splotch of reddish-brown that had seeped through to the inside lining. "The other one — "

"What about the other one?" He didn't sound like Gideon anymore . . . his voice was low and strangely hoarse. . . .

"The hand," Kate murmured, and she didn't even realize that she had taken a step back from him, away from that strange, pasty look on his face. "There was a hand inside. Only it was a joke. I'm sure it was . . . Gideon?"

"I know this," he mumbled.

"What?"

"This glove . . . it's — " Abruptly he broke off, his eyes raising to her face as if he'd just remembered she was there. "Just stay on this path — it'll take you back where we started."

"Gideon?" Kate moved toward him, but the look in his eyes stopped her.

"Just go, Kate. Go now."

And as she stood there watching helplessly, he turned and disappeared into the woods.

Chapter 9

"Don't tell me." Denzil threw up his arms as Kate ran over to the van. "You thought I said two *days*, not two hours — "

"I hope you're satisfied." Kate glared at him. "I just *hope* you're satisfied!"

"That you're here? Of *course* I'm satisfied. We're *late* and now we can *go*!"

"That's not what I meant, and you know it."

As Denzil calmly appraised her expression, he leaned back against the van with a groan. "Oh, please, why me? *Now* what?"

"Don't play so innocent, Denzil. What happened was awful."

"Oh, no." Tawney stuck her head out the door, nodding sympathetically. "You lost your watch, I bet. No wonder you're so late."

"No, I didn't lose my watch." Kate shut her eyes and counted to ten. When she opened them again, Denzil and Tawney were watching her expectantly. "You *followed* me into the woods. You *spied* on me and Gideon — "

"Spied on you and Gideon?" Denzil's eyes widened in mock alarm. "What were you and Gideon *doing*?"

"And then you planted that *stupid* glove — "

"Whoa, whoa, whoa. Uh-unh. Not this glove thing again — I can't take it — "

"You know you did it, and that I'm *on* to you! Why don't you just admit it and cut all this — "

"Go on, Tawney, tell her I didn't do it."

"Didn't do what?" Tawney's eyes widened in usual confusion. "I don't even know what you're talking about!"

"Hey" — Denzil grinned — "me neither! Kate, Tawney and I don't know what you're talking about. Now can we go?"

"I'd really like that." Tawney brightened. "Then we can have lunch that somebody else fixes for a change."

Exasperated, Kate climbed into the van beside Tawney. Denzil slid into the front, and within minutes they were bumping their way to the village. At first no one spoke, but finally Denzil gave a huge sigh that demanded Kate's attention.

"Now. What about *what* glove?"

Kate stared at his reflection in the rearview mirror. "Denzil, please. Gideon was so upset, it's nothing to joke about."

"Then tell *me* the joke." He looked so innocent that Kate felt her resolve weakening. "I'd really like to know."

Kate withdrew her accusing stare. "The glove. It was on the path when Gideon and I started back.

It looked like the one you don't believe I really saw. The one with the hand — " She bit her lip. "The one I took away from Pet by my cabin."

"Right. The severed hand." Denzil rolled his eyes.

"Yecch," said Tawney.

"Remember I told you that Gideon and I had a meeting this morning so he could critique my story? And then we took a walk — "

"Oh," Tawney sighed, "how romantic. I think Gideon is so romantic, don't you, Kate?"

"Don't you, Kate?" Denzil grinned, shifting into low gear as they maneuvered their way down a steep, winding hill.

"We were *talking* about writing," Kate said indignantly. "It was purely professional."

"Hey, I believe you." Denzil nodded. "If *anyone* believes you, it's me."

"*As* I was saying" — Kate sighed — "we ended up in the woods and then we came back, and I fell and that's when I found it — only first I thought I heard something — only Gideon looked so strange — he got so *upset* about it — "

"Whoa!" Denzil yelled. He clamped one hand down on his hat and swiveled around, trying to keep one eye on the road. "Hold it right there. Just back up and let me have it again — nice and slow-like."

So Kate took a deep breath and started all over, and by the time they reached town, Denzil and Tawney were as perplexed as she was.

"It's weird, all right," Denzil agreed, pulling into a parking lot behind a small grocery store. "That glove must have some kind of meaning to Gideon for him to act that way."

"He said he knew it," Kate said seriously. "Whatever that means. He really wanted me out of there in a hurry."

"Maybe he had to go to the bathroom." Tawney nodded. "That always makes me want to hurry."

"Right. Gloves just affect some guys that way." Denzil leaned his forehead against the steering wheel. "Jeez, Tawney — "

"He did look kind of sick." Kate placated her. "His whole face went white."

"Probably expensive gloves," Denzil said, trying not to smile. "Made him sick thinking of all that money down the drain."

"And what about the sounds I heard?" Kate persisted.

"What about them? It was probably just some animal." Denzil thought a minute. "Probably the same animal that ate your swimsuit. He has your scent now, and you don't have a chance. Wherever you go, he'll be following . . . waiting to rip off your clothes."

"Denzil — "

"Okay, forget I said that." Denzil jumped from the van, clapping his hands. "Who gets groceries and who goes to the post office and who — ?"

"You pick up the mail," Tawney said. "And Kate and I will get what we need and meet you in an hour."

"An hour." Denzil looked dubious. "That's an hour, Kate. Sixty minutes. High noon."

Kate jerked his hat down over his eyes. "I'll see if I can manage it, *hombre.*"

The shopping went faster than expected, so the girls loaded up the van and went off in search of Denzil to have lunch. They finally found him talking to the attendant at the gas station, and as the three of them set off for the drugstore, Denzil suddenly stopped and pointed.

"Look — the creature walks among us."

They ducked into a doorway as Pearce came around the corner, his arms loaded with boxes. Unaware that he was being watched, he loaded the pickup at the curb, then went back the way he'd come.

"Why are we hiding?" Kate asked, annoyed.

"Because we're spying on him." Denzil grinned.

"Why are we spying on him?"

" 'Cause it's fun."

"I think he's handsome," Tawney sighed. "Even if he *does* make me feel creepy."

Denzil cast her a reproachful look. "You think *everyone's* handsome."

"That's not true." Tawney sounded offended. "I don't think *you're* handsome."

Kate burst out laughing, but Denzil grabbed her arm.

"Ssh — here he comes again."

They watched as Pearce reappeared and loaded a second armful of boxes onto the bed of the truck.

"He's just picking up supplies like he always does," Tawney sighed. "I don't know what's so interesting about that."

"How do you know it's supplies?" Denzil asked out of the corner of his mouth. "How do you know it's not surgical instruments . . . or pieces of his victims. . . ."

"Look." Kate shushed them and pulled farther back into cover. "Something's happening."

As they refocused their attention on the sidewalk, a car veered to the curb, brakes squealing as it slammed to a halt. Pearce stepped back, frowning, and a second later the car door flung open as Gideon burst out.

"Oh, dear," Tawney whispered. "He looks really upset."

"I wish I could hear what they're saying." Denzil craned his neck, but Kate jerked him back.

Gideon *did* look upset. As the three friends watched in dismay, he advanced on Pearce, backing him up against a wall, his voice raising as he shoved something into Pearce's face. For a moment Pearce stared, expressionless, then slowly reached out and took it from Gideon.

Squinting to see, Kate saw Pearce lift the thing up into the sunlight . . . and felt her own breath catch in her throat.

It was a brown glove.

Forgetting caution, she inched closer, scarcely aware of Denzil's grip on her shirt, yanking her back. Pearce was talking now, in low, even tones, and the look on Gideon's face was frightened — almost desperate. And then, to their amazement, Pearce caught Gideon's shoulders in a quick hug and hurried him back into his car. A second later Pearce jumped into the pickup and followed Gideon out of sight.

"Well, I'll be." Denzil stepped out into the sunlight. "Whaddya know about that."

"Why, I just think that's so sweet." Tawney's eyes misted. "Gideon was so upset, and Pearce was really caring about him." She thought a moment as Denzil and Kate stared at her. "Let's not ever tell him we saw. He might get embarrassed."

"Good idea," Denzil agreed. "Let's go." He herded them down the sidewalk and into the drugstore. "I'm plumb starved — I could eat a horse."

Kate glanced at him in surprise. For someone who'd been so eager to spy, he seemed suspiciously uninterested now. She waited till they sat down and ordered and Tawney went to find a bathroom before she confronted him.

"Okay, Denzil. You're being awfully casual about all this."

"Wait." He shot a glance around the room. "I don't want Tawney hearing anything. She'll have nightmares the rest of her natural life."

Kate leaned over and gazed at his frown. "What's up?"

"What's up?" he echoed. "That was the glove, wasn't it? The one you told me about — the one you accused *me* of leaving there."

Kate nodded reluctantly. "I think so. I mean, from what I could see, I'm pretty sure it was. Denzil, Gideon looked *beside* himself — if you really *did* plant that glove, you'd better say so because something is *very* wrong here."

"You're telling me?" Denzil bent forward, his head practically touching hers. "Why would a glove cause such a crisis? Huh? You tell me why one little glove would make somebody come apart the way Gideon was coming apart back there."

"Because . . ." — Kate's shoulders lifted in a slow shrug — "he lost it? He's been looking for it for a long time?"

"What if it's *not* his?"

A strange feeling of unease was creeping along the back of her neck. "Someone *else* lost it?"

"William."

Kate's heart exploded, sending chills racing along her arms. "God, Denzil, what are you saying?"

"I'm saying maybe it's William's glove, and William's missing. Didn't Gideon recognize it right before he told you to leave?"

"Yes, but — "

"Jeez, Kate, think about it. He drives all the way here, looking for Pearce — they have a *scene* — Pearce *leaves* with him — all because Gideon holds up that glove."

Kate leaned back against the booth, suddenly weak. "It had stains on it."

This time it was Denzil who looked uncomfortable. "It's a work glove. It's supposed to have stains on it."

"No, this was different. This was dark, and there'd been a lot of it." She reached out for her water, fingers trembling around the glass. "Then . . . what you're saying is — "

"What I'm saying is that it's *weird!*" Denzil

squirmed, his voice almost angry. "*That's* what I'm saying — "

"That something happened to William — "

"Kate." Denzil shook his head warningly.

"That maybe he's disappeared because he's *dead* — "

"Ssh — here comes Tawney — "

"That — oh, God, Denzil — " She clutched his arm, fear brimming in her eyes. "Then that glove — that Pet had in her mouth — "

"Come on, Kate, don't do this — "

"Was really . . . William Drewe's hand."

Denzil stared at her, his expression grim. "If it was," he whispered, "where's the rest of him?"

Chapter 10

"Well, I don't know why you two couldn't eat, and now you're being so quiet — I think we had a *wonderful* day." Tawney beamed.

Behind the steering wheel Denzil grunted. "Oh, you betcha. And seeing Pearce and Gideon just gave it that perfect touch."

Tawney's eyes went wide with concern, his sarcasm lost on her. "I felt sorry for Gideon. Maybe he'd even been crying or something, the way he was waving his handkerchief around."

Without thinking, Kate mumbled, "That wasn't a handkerchief, Tawney, it was a — "

"Wallet!" Denzil shouted. "At least," his voice lowered, "it looked like a wallet."

"Well, I don't know, I couldn't see that far, anyway." Tawney sighed. "Maybe he needs money . . . Poor Gideon, I hope more people take classes from him if he needs money."

"And speaking of classes, Denzil" — Kate kept her eyes on the passing scenery — "why didn't you tell me you took a class with Gideon before? I hear you were quite the troublemaker."

"Did *he* tell you that?" Denzil snorted. "Don't believe everything you hear — especially from Gideon Drewe."

"I remember that," Tawney spoke up. "Didn't he tell you that all your stories were predictable, and that there wasn't any suspense, and that you couldn't scare anybody and — "

"Tawney," Denzil muttered between clenched teeth.

"What?"

"Just . . . shut . . . up."

"Oh. Okay."

Denzil gunned the engine, urging the van up the hillside. Tawney closed her eyes, humming to herself. Kate stared into her own thoughts, a confused jumble of darkness. . . . The next thing she knew, Tawney was shaking her arm.

"Kate?"

She looked up into Tawney's worried face.

"Kate, are you okay? We're home now."

"Gosh, I must have dozed off." Kate shook her head, trying to clear it, and began handing supplies out the door to Denzil. "Gideon's supposed to have a class this afternoon — are you going?"

Denzil swung the bags to the kitchen porch and wouldn't look at her. "Reckon I'll have to miss this one. I'm on grub duty."

"I'll take notes for you then." Kate reached out and brushed his arm, relieved when he nodded.

"Much obliged." He grinned as she started back to her cabin.

She was already reaching for her purse when she remembered she still didn't have a key. Grumbling, she gave the doorknob an irritated twist and was surprised when it opened.

"Miss Bunceton?" Peering into the cabin, Kate caught her breath and clutched at the wall.

Someone had been in here, but it hadn't been her teacher.

And there had been only one victim in mind.

Everything in Kate's half of the room had been ransacked, her suitcase emptied out, contents strewn wildly about. Clothes had been flung everywhere, some of them ripped, and as she stared in growing horror at her bed she saw long slash marks through her pillow. The thick silence was suddenly dangerous. As she slowly backed away she realized that the bathroom light was on, and something bright red gleamed at her from just beyond the door. . . .

"Oh, God . . ."

She froze, her heart straining. *I'll go get Denzil . . . I'll call the police . . . Gideon will know what to do. . . .* But instead she felt herself drawn by a horrible curiosity, drawn helplessly to the bathroom door, her breath choking her, her hands pressed to her mouth to hold back her panic. . . .

Blood.

Blood was everywhere . . . splattered on the walls . . . the tile . . . dripping from the sink . . . smeared in wide, greasy arcs across the floor. . . .

The door to the shower stall was closed. Dark stains spread out from beneath it, already congealing into thick, puddinglike masses upon the soaked rug.

As Kate's eyes fell upon the mirror, she saw herself looking back, her pale, frightened face framed by long slashes of red. . . .

And beneath her face . . . just beneath her red-slashed reflection, the savagely scribbled words:

TEACHER'S PET

For one split second the room swayed around her, throbbing red, the scent of death thick in her throat. Kate backed up slowly, feeling behind her for the door, and when she felt herself stumble back out onto the porch, she turned and ran all the way to the kitchen.

"*Denzil!*"

Looking up from the stove, Denzil saluted as Kate burst through the door. "Hey! Long time no — whoa!"

Kate pulled him out the back door, out of earshot of the kitchen crew. "Denzil, hurry, someone's been in my room — "

A joke formed on Denzil's lips, then froze there as he studied Kate's face. "You're serious."

"Of *course* I'm serious! There's blood all over — they messed up my stuff — there's a message on the bathroom mirror — "

"What?"

"Don't tell Tawney. Don't tell anyone yet. I don't know what to do!"

"Okay, calm down. Let's take a look."

"But can you leave? Don't you have to work? I just — "

"Hey, Tawney." Denzil stuck his head back inside the door. "I've gotta get something over at the lodge. I'll be right back." He closed the door with a jaunty wave, then grabbed Kate's arm, practically pulling her down the road. "Is anything missing? Did they steal anything?"

"I didn't even check. I remembered I didn't have a key, but the door was open when I got there. I think there might be something in the shower!"

"Do you think Miss B left it unlocked for you, and someone just came in?"

"No, all our things are in there. I don't think she'd do that."

"Is any of *her* stuff stolen?"

"They didn't even *touch* her stuff. Just mine. Oh, please, hurry — "

They didn't start running until they were well out of sight of the road. When they reached the cabin, Denzil went in first, staring openmouthed at the confusion.

"In here." Kate pushed him into the bathroom, holding her nose against the smell. Despite his shocked reaction, she felt a little safer now with both their faces reflected there in the mirror. Denzil's incredulous gaze swept over the room, then fixed on the words smeared across the glass.

"A jealous colleague? What the hell does it mean?"

"I don't know. I think there might be something in there." She pointed to the shower stall, then stepped away as Denzil cautiously inched open the door.

"God . . ."

"Oh, Denzil, what is it? Is someone — ?"

He backed out, shaking his head. "There's nothing in there, Kate."

"Nothing? But I don't — "

"*Something* was in there, but it's gone now."

"Let me see — "

"No." He put his hands on her shoulders, pushing her gently back against the sink again. "It looks like something was killed in there. Like an animal. Like something was killed . . . and then . . . just drained. I've never seen so much blood."

"I think I'm going to throw up."

"Be my guest." Denzil nodded, and as Kate sank down in a limp heap on the floor, he wet a washrag under the faucet and handed it to her.

"It's the smell," Kate gasped, holding the cloth over her nose. "Don't you smell that?"

"You mean the blood? That real metallic smell — "

"No, it's something else. Besides the blood — I . . . I can't place it." Kate lowered her head, fighting off a wave of dizziness. "It's horrible. Denzil . . . what is going on?"

Regarding the mirror, Denzil scratched his jaw.

"Is it a warning maybe? Someone doesn't like your writing? Well, I'll tell you what, whoever it is, is one hell of a critic."

Staring at him, Kate suddenly burst out laughing, the sound bordering on hysteria. "Will you be *serious*?"

He knelt slowly beside her. "Okay, it can basically mean one thing, right? Someone doesn't like the attention you've been getting from Gideon. *Right*?"

"No." Kate shook her head. "I don't think that's — "

"Come on, he singled you out in class, he raved about your story, he took you for a walk — "

"But it doesn't make sense. I mean, so *what* if he pays attention to me? Everyone here's an adult; we're not talking about some grade-school crush or something. I haven't noticed anyone displaying any over-affection for the teacher, have you? Or anyone who seems demented — "

"Who knows what someone might be thinking, Kate? You can't always tell a crazy person by his face."

"So you really think a *crazy* person did this?" She looked startled.

Denzil chuckled. "Well, this isn't something *I* enjoy doing myself . . . you know, destroying a girl's room, sacrificing some animal in her shower, writing clichés on her mirror in blood — "

"Then this proves it," Kate said flatly.

"What proves what?"

"Last night when Tawney and I were swimming.

I *told* you someone was on the bank watching me. It was deliberate, don't you see? They took my key and cut up my clothes."

Denzil's smile faded. He looked again at the mirror.

"Why is someone after me, Denzil?" Kate looked so beseeching that he took her hand. "I don't know anyone here. I haven't done anything or — "

"Okay, okay, let's look at it another way. It might just be someone's idea of a joke, though what possible humor they find in all this is beyond me. Still" — Denzil sighed — "there are lots of real sickos out there in the world."

A sudden knock sounded on the cabin door, and they both jumped. As Denzil held his finger to his lips, Kate backed up, holding her breath while he peeked cautiously out into the room.

"It's Pearce," he hissed back over his shoulder. "He's coming in." Denzil flattened himself against the wall behind the door as Kate hurried out into the other room.

"What are you doing here?" she demanded. "Do you always just go around barging into people's cabins?"

Pearce froze in the doorway, his dark eyes sliding from Kate to the chaos thrown around the room. For one brief instant Kate thought she saw a flicker of something — *what?* — *surprise?* — *alarm?*

"What happened in here?" His voice was cold as steel, and Kate felt her own voice quiver as his eyes settled on her again.

"I found it like this," she said. "When I came back to my cabin just now."

Pearce was still staring, not saying a word. After an endless stretch of silence he asked, "Anyone hurt?"

"No."

"Anything stolen?"

"I don't think so."

He nodded slowly, his eyes flickering to the closed bathroom door. "Have you been in there?"

"Yes. It's just this room."

Pearce's black eyes crawled slowly across the clutter . . . up the walls . . . across the floor. His hand stretched out toward her. "Here's your key. Try not to lose it this time. I'll bring you some new bedding."

Kate took the key from his fingers, felt the hidden strength in his upturned palm.

"It happens," Pearce said quietly. "Vandalism. The cabins get broken into all the time. I'll report it . . . but it happens."

Kate said nothing, just watched him turn and go out the door. She watched as he slipped down onto the path and was surprised when he turned around again.

His deep eyes fastened on her, and his voice was as unreadable as his face. At his side one hand slowly tightened into a fist.

"If I were you," he said, "I'd be very careful."

Trembling, Kate pressed her hand to her eyes.

When she looked again, the path was empty.

Chapter 11

Bad surprises.

I heard you say it, Kate . . . back there in the woods.

You like to be scared. . . .

But not by bad surprises.

So this was only a little bit bad. . . .

Because the worst is yet to come.

Teacher's pet . . .

Teacher's pet . . .

You're going to die . . .

But not . . . just . . . yet.

Chapter 12

After the strange encounter she'd seen in the village earlier, Kate was surprised to see Gideon in class that afternoon. He was perched on the edge of a desk when she walked in, sunlight slanting across his bent head, his face strained as he studied his watch. When everyone was seated, he stared a moment out the window, then glanced thoughtfully at Pet, curled beside him.

"Fear," he began quietly, "seldom plays fair. Its best weapon is often surprise. Often, distortion. Always . . . the unknown."

Once more Kate felt helplessly drawn by the spell of his voice, and she closed her eyes to listen.

"Perhaps the unknown we fear most is ourselves — our darker sides. We don't like to be reminded of what that darker side can do. We fear it turning on us without warning. Taking over. Changing us from something human to something totally evil. Stalking us. Watching . . . waiting for its chance to pounce."

Yawning, Pet arched herself against Gideon's side and stretched regally down again, surveying the roomful of startled faces with something akin to disdain.

"This afternoon," Gideon went on, "we're going to be working with another fear technique. Descriptions. Creating certain moods and communicating through our senses. I compiled a list at home last night, assigning each of you a particular spot around camp that I feel offers special atmosphere. I've also posted a list in the lodge, in case anyone should need to find you this afternoon for any reason. What I want you to do is write a description of your assigned location. It must be both physical and emotional — and through that description, I want you to make the reader *feel* what you yourself are experiencing. You can drop your papers off here when you're finished, and I'll collect them after dinner. In the meanwhile, I'll be in the lodge if you need me."

As students got their instructions and eagerly set out, Kate lagged behind, gathering her things together and waiting for the room to empty. The memory of her ransacked cabin still clung to her like a nightmare; between her and Denzil and some heavy-duty cleaning supplies, they'd finally gotten the bathroom back to normal, though Denzil swore the smell of blood still lingered there. Now she closed her eyes, forcing the horrible images away, and when she opened them again, Gideon was staring at her from across the deserted room.

"Kate?"

She offered him a tentative smile. "I just wanted to make sure . . . are you okay?"

Her concern seemed to catch him off guard. "Why, of course, thank you for asking. Is there . . . some reason I shouldn't be?"

Kate looked away. *Because you looked half out of your mind in the village, don't you remember . . . ?* "You seemed so upset on our walk this morning."

"That was rude of me," Gideon said quietly. "I suddenly remembered an important engagement, but that doesn't excuse my behavior. Am I forgiven?"

She nodded slowly, still seeing that stricken look on his face . . . still seeing the glove. . . . "I don't suppose there's been any news of William?"

"Why do you ask?" Gideon's eyes rested upon hers with a calm intensity, but one hand froze midair above the cat's head. Pet rolled over on her side and swatted at his finger, leaving a pencil-line scratch that Gideon didn't seem to feel.

"It's just that you must be so worried," she said carefully.

Was it her imagination, or did something shudder through Gideon, tensing his muscles, darkening his eyes? As Kate stared, the expression seemed to freeze upon his face, and his smile seemed strangely painted.

"Well, you needn't worry about William, he does

this sort of thing quite a lot." One hand absently descended . . . stroked Pet's back. "I've no doubt he'll turn up. Life can't come to a halt because of him, now, can it?"

As Kate watched, his other hand groped for a piece of paper on the desk.

"You're waiting for your assignment, of course."

"No, actually — "

"You'll like this one," Gideon cut in, handing her the paper. "I tried to think of a place you'd particularly enjoy. It's a bit off the main route, but you can see it easily from the trail."

Kate accepted the paper, feeling slightly hurt at his sudden change in tone. "Sounds like fun," she said lamely.

He stood and began collecting his papers. As Kate silently turned to go, his fingers suddenly closed around her elbow. "Kate . . ." His hand raised slowly . . . reached out . . . lightly touched the hair on her forehead. "You're really so extraordinary, you know . . . so extraordinary that . . . it frightens me — "

Breaking off, his eyes fastened on the doorway behind her, and Kate started to turn in the direction of his stare.

"What is it? What's wrong?"

"Nothing." His hands were on her shoulders, paralyzed, and Kate winced from their unexpected strength.

"Ouch, Gideon, you're hurting me — "

"I'm sorry." And suddenly his voice was distracted, his body moving quickly toward the door. "Forgive me, Kate, but I'm afraid something has come up."

"Gideon?" Puzzled, Kate watched him leave, Pet following behind. By the time she reached the door herself, she saw Gideon standing with Pearce on the other side of the road. They seemed to be arguing about something, and Gideon kept looking off into the woods. Spying Kate there outside the cabin, he said something to Pearce, and they went into the lodge. Shrugging, Kate looked down at her assignment and started walking, then heard Miss Bunceton's familiar shout.

"Yoo-hoo! Kate! Where are you off to, dear?"

"A writing project." Kate waved back, and as she explained the exercise, Miss Bunceton fluttered in delight.

"Well, it sounds perfectly marvelous! Would you mind if I came along? I could do with some inspiration myself."

Kate didn't see how she could get much accomplished in Miss Bunceton's company, but since there didn't seem to be any gracious way of refusing, she gave in.

"I don't know where this place is — Drewe's Cave. Somewhere past the lake."

"But you have a map there, I see. Come, dear, we'll surely find it."

Hiding a smile, Kate led the way, only half listening as Miss Bunceton kept up a constant stream of talk. She was relieved when the woman finally spied a shady little hollow that piqued her interest.

"Can't you just see it, Kate?" Miss Bunceton breathed deeply. "The wounded hero lying there, suffering, while the heroine ministers to his needs?" As Kate shook her head in amusement, the woman added, "A stoic hero, mind you — one who would *never* want his weaknesses and vulnerabilities known to a *woman*!"

Kate laughed and pointed ahead to the ongoing trail. "If you're going to stay, I'll just pick you up on my way back."

"Wonderful. Who knows? I may have a whole novel written by the time we meet again."

"X-rated, I hope," Kate shot back, and could still hear Miss Bunceton hooting with laughter as she disappeared from view.

After several more minutes Kate began to wonder if she'd somehow taken the wrong trail. She hadn't seen any other people on this route, and the heavy silence was almost suffocating. Stopping to rest, she studied her map again, then leaned against a tree and closed her eyes.

And then . . . slowly . . . the skin began to prickle along her arms.

Kate's eyes flew open, a cry catching in her throat.

For one horrible instant she'd had the overpowering feeling that she was being watched.

Quickly her eyes scanned the trail . . . the woods, so thick, so mottled with colors and shadows.

Kate . . . Kate . . . doomed to your fate. . . .

Teacher's pet.

Looking back over her shoulder, Kate set off

again, walking faster. She could see it now, the narrow pathway spiraling downwards from the main trail, leading to a spindly-bare thicket and the yawning mouth of a cave. Gideon was certainly right about atmosphere, Kate thought grimly, starting down — the place had a sinister, almost hopeless look about it. She hesitated several feet from the cave entrance, took a deep breath, and moved forward.

She stood for a moment in a pool of light. A canopy of leaves settled behind her as she pushed through, daylight closing off with a soft rustling. The gaping entry was clotted with weeds and rubble, fanned by a damp, invisible breeze. Ahead of her the light grew weaker and weaker, until it finally faded altogether, swallowed by the black depths of the cave. Kate stared hard into that blackness, wondering what lay beyond. . . .

And saw someone staring back at her.

With a cry, her eyes fixed in disbelief on the black eyes that pulled slowly out of the shadows. Pearce separated himself from the darkness and stood in front of her.

"What are you *doing* here?!" Kate pressed one hand to her racing heart, backing farther away from him.

Pearce regarded her thoughtfully for several seconds. The only thing that moved were his eyes, sliding down the front of her . . . returning to her face.

"Just my job," he said, shrugging.

"And what kind of job is that — hiding and scaring me half to death?"

"Oh." One eyebrow raised. "I thought you liked to be scared." And then, as Kate stared at him, "At least that's what Gideon tells me."

Unnerved, Kate struggled to keep her voice calm. "I . . . I wish you'd just leave. I'm supposed to do a writing assignment here."

"Ah." Pearce nodded. "So you're the one who has the cave."

"How do you know about that?"

"I helped him make up the list. I know the area better than he does."

Kate felt weak. "But . . . you didn't assign — "

"The places to the people?" His eyes were amused. "Gideon's the teacher . . . not me."

"So there's no reason for you to be here." Kate took another step back. "I can't write when someone's watching me."

"You should be glad I have a good memory." Pearce jerked his chin toward the blackness behind him. "It's a favorite spot for copperheads. I've found nests back there before."

Her stomach tightened but she looked back, undaunted. "I wouldn't have gone back in there."

"Well" — he gave the slightest nod — "then I guess there's no problem."

"Wait — " She glanced into the cave, searching the floor, the piles of fallen rock, seeing nothing. "Did you . . . find any?"

The smile was cold . . . mocking . . . crawling

slowly across his lips. His eyes held hers for an endless moment, and then he started forward.

Kate heard the awful sounds before she realized what was happening. . . .

The sudden, horrible crunching . . . the scream of pain and surprise as Pearce went down . . . the thud of his head against stone. . . .

And as Kate got to him and knelt by his side, she saw the steel trap clamped around his foot, hidden there in the tall weeds.

Chapter 13

"Pearce?" Kate stared in horror at his unconscious form sprawled there on the ground. "Pearce? Can you hear me?" Panicky, she grabbed at the trap, her eyes desperately sweeping over their surroundings. "Pearce! Wake up!"

To her relief, his eyes fluttered open, fixing on her face in dazed confusion. For one awful moment Kate thought he was going to pass out again, but then he moaned and stiffened, his face draining white.

"Oh, God!" Kate stared helplessly as Pearce writhed beside her, his hands uselessly clutching the metal jaws that held him fast. "Oh, God, what can I do? Tell me what to *do*!"

"Get — get Gideon — " The words came from between clenched teeth, and though every instinct in her wanted to run, Kate stubbornly shook her head.

"I'm not leaving you here alone. We've got to get this thing off your leg — you've got to help me." She was surprised that her words even got through to him. Gasping, he rolled over and took hold of the trap, his fingers slippery with blood.

"You'll have . . . to pull," his breath choked out. "You'll have — to — pull hard — "

"Yes, yes, I'll pull, just show me what to do."

Kate's hands were shaking as much as her voice, and she prayed for calm, terrified she'd accidentally let go before he could pull free. With every muscle straining, she grabbed one side of the trap and worked it steadily outward, her frightened eyes on Pearce, who looked like he might faint again at any second. Scarcely daring to breathe, she saw his foot pull inch by inch out of danger, and she used her last ounce of strength to ease the trap slowly back into place. Pearce fell back, exhausted, his face a pasty mask.

"Just lie still — take deep breaths — I'm going to try and stop the bleeding now, okay?"

"Just — go away. Leave me alone."

"Don't talk, save your strength." Kate shrugged out of her jacket and wrapped it around him, shocked at the wetness of his clothes, the coldness of his skin. Beneath his injured leg the ground was staining dark. Gritting her teeth, Kate eased off his shoe, gently pushed up the leg of his jeans, and rolled off his sock. The ripped flesh and exposed bone almost made her swoon, but she managed a shaky smile at him over her shoulder. "Well . . . it could be worse. . . ."

"Help me up."

"You're not going anywhere. Don't even think about it."

As Pearce moved his leg, a look of pure anguish contorted his face and again he fell back, stunned. "Jesus . . ."

"Just be still and don't talk," Kate said again, more firmly this time. "Do you have a handkerchief? Anything?"

He nodded distractedly and pulled a rag from his back pocket. Kate bit her lip and applied the rag carefully, tying it above the wound, wincing at the expression on his face.

"I'm not going to leave you. My teacher — Miss Bunceton — is just down the trail. When I don't come back, she'll either start looking for me, or she'll send help. Anyway, someone's bound to be here soon."

Another vague nod. As a chill raced through his body, Kate tucked the jacket tighter around his shoulders and sat down beside him, pressing close.

"Does your head hurt? It looked like you hit pretty hard when you fell — we have to make sure you stay awake, okay?" When he didn't answer, she touched his arm, trying to focus his attention on her. "I can't believe somebody set that trap — just left it here like that — someone could have been — "

Biting her lip, she left the sentence unfinished, leaning down to scrutinize him. He was trembling all over. He turned his face away, and his voice was husky.

"You'd like to believe that, wouldn't you?"

Startled, Kate pulled back, her hand falling from his arm. "Believe what?"

A long silence passed. Pearce tensed at a fresh wave of pain. "Do you really think this was an accident?" His head moved toward her; to Kate's alarm more color drained from his too-white cheeks. "Do you really think this was meant for me?"

A slow dread crawled through her, and she peered urgently into his face. "What . . . what are you talking about?"

Pearce didn't answer. He shifted his eyes away from her, gazing numbly at the trees.

Loosening the tourniquet, Kate berated herself for not having gone for help right away. The sun was slipping behind the trees, and the wind was biting cold. Surely Miss Bunceton had gotten concerned by now and gone for help. Surely when Kate didn't return to camp, Gideon would get worried and come looking for her. If she left now, she could get there before dark — *and maybe Pearce won't fall asleep, maybe he doesn't have a concussion, maybe he won't pass out* —

"Careful," he mumbled. "You have to be . . . so careful. . . ."

Startled, Kate glanced down to see Pearce's eyes on her, glazed even darker with pain. She stared at him, wondering if he'd slipped into shock or was hallucinating.

"Careful? What do you mean?"

There was no answer. A gust of wind swept down from the woods.

"I'm cold," Pearce whispered.

Alarmed, Kate eased down beside him, stretching her body along his. She couldn't feel any warmth from him anywhere.

"You're going to be okay," she whispered. "I promise."

He tried to shift his position . . . gave a soft moan. Kate's heart ached at the sound, and she lay one arm carefully across his chest. Slowly his head turned until his midnight-black eyes were inches from her own, their agony holding her so that she couldn't look away.

"Kate . . ." he mumbled.

"Yes?" And she was holding him closer, trying not to cry. "What can I do? Just tell me."

"I . . ." His voice was low, so low that she could hardly hear. "I don't . . . want anything . . . to happen to you."

She found his lips . . . and they were so cold . . . so unresponsive . . . yet as she kissed him, his hand moved upon her back . . . beneath her sweater . . . against her bare skin . . . trying to hold her with strength he didn't have.

"It's all right," she whispered. "It's going to be all right. . . ." And she felt his heart against hers . . . and she wished more than anything that she could take all his suffering away. . . .

"Kate!" The voice drifted through the trees, echoed by other voices, startling Pearce and Kate and splitting them apart. Flustered, Kate jumped up and shouted back.

"Yes! Yes! I'm here! Pearce is with me, and he's hurt!"

She could see the lights then, flashlights and lanterns bobbing down the hill, and in another few seconds, the area was swarming with people, and Gideon was there, gathering her into his arms.

"Good Lord, Kate, we thought the worst. What in the world — ?"

"He got caught in a trap." Confused, Kate wanted to pull away, out of Gideon's arms, but they were so strong . . . so safe. "I was coming here to write, and he was checking the cave and the next thing I knew — "

"Pearce?" Gideon cut her off, kneeling beside Pearce and lowering the lantern close to the injured foot. Even in the half-light Kate could see his face struggling for composure. "It looks like he's lost a lot of blood. We'll have to carry him back and get him to a doctor. Careful now — don't hurt him."

"Gideon — when he fell, he hit his head against that rock — that's why I was afraid to leave him — "

"I'm so sorry, Kate. This must have been terrifying for you." Gideon looked down at the tourniquet, his expression grateful. "Thank God you knew what to do for him."

Kate stood back, the whole scene playing out before her like a dream. She saw several of the men make a chair with their arms and carry Pearce away; she saw Gideon stand for several long moments, staring down at the trap, his features finally contorting in fury.

"Damn!" He kicked the trap so hard that it hit the rocks, bouncing back with a clatter. As Kate jumped away, she saw Denzil and Tawney hovering a few feet behind her, not sure whether to approach or not. Gideon's hands knotted into fists, his voice shaking with quiet rage. "Who could have done this? Who could have done such a thing?"

Catching his breath, he spun on his heel and stalked away, leaving Kate to gaze after him.

"Kate, are you all right?"

Denzil and Tawney ran up then, catching Kate between them in a gigantic hug.

"I'm okay," Kate said weakly, "But Pearce . . . it's so awful. I wanted to get help but . . ." She bit her lip, trying not to think about what had happened, and in the dim light, spotted something shiny on the ground. "What's that?"

Denzil glanced down, disinterested. "Looks like a watch to me."

"It must be Gideon's." Kate retrieved it and shoved it into her pocket. "He must have dropped it when he was helping Pearce — "

"Oh, Kate!" Tawney flung her arms around her friend again. "You're so brave! I wouldn't have known what to do!"

"Yeah, well, let's get back and warm you up." Denzil shrugged out of his jacket and put it around Kate, the three of them heading back for the trail. "If it hadn't been for Miss B, you'd probably still be here."

"I *knew* she'd go for help," Kate said gratefully. "I knew she'd miss me sooner or later."

"It was later," Denzil laughed. "And the only reason she came back to camp is 'cause she sat in poison ivy. You were almost an afterthought."

"I should have known. Is she okay?"

"Not really. She's got the most beautiful rash you've ever seen, and she's swollen twice her size."

"That's big." Tawney nodded solemnly.

"We had to take her to the clinic in the village," Denzil went on. "I don't reckon you'll have a roommate for a while."

Kate caught his meaningful look, which Tawney couldn't see. Her body ached from cold, and she felt dead tired. There was so much she had to think about, to sort out, but right now her brain just wouldn't function.

" — eat," Denzil was saying. "Come on there, kid, you're lagging behind." He flung one arm around her shoulder and squeezed her to his side. "Hot chowder and homemade bread and lots of strong coffee and — "

"I'm not hungry," Kate said, smiling her thanks. "I just want a nice hot shower right now."

"Okay, but you don't know what you're missing."

As they approached the lodge, Kate saw the truck take off toward the village, and she stood there watching, a strange, empty feeling inside.

"Hey, you sure you're okay?" Denzil asked softly, and Kate pulled her attention back with an effort. "Sure you won't change your mind?"

"Thanks, but I just want to get out of these damp things."

"Anything happen back there I should know about?"

Kate's hands lifted to her burning cheeks, and

she was glad for the darkness. "No. I mean, he wasn't particularly terrifying, lying there caught in that trap."

"Okay. Come back when you're changed."

She gave him a vacant nod, handing his jacket back, and squeezed Tawney's hand good-bye. Then slowly she made her way to her cabin, two images pounding mercilessly in her mind:

Pearce's lips . . . exploring hers so tenderly in the dark. . . .

And Pearce's voice. *"I don't want anything to happen to you."*

Chapter 14

Kate leaned in the cabin doorway, surveying her room. Everything was just as she'd left it with things straightened and returned to their places. There was a new pillow on her bed.

Walking cautiously to the bathroom, she flicked on the light and gazed at her reflection in the clean mirror. She looked haggard, and there were dark circles under her eyes.

Turning on the heater, she knelt beside it, holding her palms toward the glowing coils. Night lay black beyond the windows, seeping cold through the thin walls. She stared down at her shirt and saw Pearce's blood still smeared there. Fighting down a wave of nausea, she threw off her clothes and heard something clatter to the floor.

Gideon's pocket watch.

Sinking onto the edge of the bed, she turned the watch over in her hand and saw that it had some sort of inscription on the back. She held it to the light, squinted at the tiny lettering, then felt her breath catch in her throat.

To Gideon . . . Love, Rowena.

"Rowena!"

Immediately the eerie meeting came back to her . . . the black-veiled figure . . . the ominous rhymes. . . . *"Kate . . . Kate . . . doomed to your fate. . . ."*

"Rowena," she mumbled again. She'd put it out of her mind after hearing Gideon speak of William's odd crowd . . . she'd just assumed . . . *what?* That William's friends had heard Gideon say how talented she was . . . or that he liked her more than a teacher might care about a promising student? That Rowena's bizarre rhymes had been nothing more than a macabre game? Except now, as Kate stared down at the inscription, she realized it really *must* have been a game — a joke on her — and maybe she'd been assuming too much.

Cheeks burning, Kate hurried into the shower, turning on the water as hot as she could stand it. *God, Kate, you're so stupid! Stupid to think Gideon really singled you out — that he thought you were special — and all this time—Rowena! She's not William's girlfriend at all — she's Gideon's — and how they must be laughing at you now. . . .*

Leaning her head against the wall, Kate took deep breaths, remembering Gideon's eyes . . . Gideon's kisses . . . and Pearce . . . Pearce watching her . . . "you have to be so careful . . . I don't want anything to happen to you." *Pearce* must have seen what was happening, her infatuation with Gideon — *he's probably seen it happen so many, many times before. . . .*

She got dressed, not really planning to go back to the kitchen and call Denzil away from his dishwashing.

"Hey, you *did* change your mind! I thought you might — lucky for you I saved some — "

"No." Kate stopped him. "I'm not hungry. I just wondered if you could tell me something."

"Have you been crying?" Denzil scrutinized her closely.

"Of course I haven't been crying — what do you think I do, fall apart just because of a little accident?"

"Okay, okay." He stepped back, hands raised. "Don't go sidewinder on me. Back! Back!"

Kate tried to gather her emotions. "Do you know where Gideon lives?" *I found it accidentally; I'd never find it again.*

"Yeah, I told you, upstate some — "

"No, I mean here. You said it's back in the woods."

"Yeah . . . but they don't like visitors. I could get fired."

"I'm not asking you to show me. Just tell me."

"Why?" Denzil's eyes narrowed suspiciously. "Don't tell me you and Gideon have some kind of rendezvous tonight."

"No, we don't, and that's dumb of you to even think. I just . . . want to return something."

"What?"

"Denzil, will you just *tell* me and stop asking all these — "

"Not that watch." He folded his arms, cocking his head at her. "Kate, that is *lame*. You could just give it to him tomorrow in class. Besides, he probably won't even be home — he went to the clinic with Pearce."

"I know where he went. Just please tell me — "

"What are you up to?"

"Nothing! Now will you just — "

"Jeez. . . ." Denzil hung his apron on the door and steered her outside. "Come on, I'll take you — but if I get in trouble — "

"I don't *want* you to go with me. Read my lips."

"Kate, you're acting like Tawney," Denzil sighed impatiently. "That *really* makes me nervous."

"It's private." Kate glared at him. "Okay, Gideon *asked* me to come. And I lost the directions. He wants to . . . loan me some books."

"Books."

"That's right."

"Let me see the watch."

"Denzil, forget about the watch, just — "

"Where is it? Here in your blouse?"

"Will you stop!"

As Kate twisted away from him, she felt his hand slide smoothly into the pocket of her jeans and withdraw again. Biting her lip, she watched as he held the watch in his upturned palm and slowly turned it over. After another second, he handed it back to her and she snatched it away.

"Kate," Denzil said sensibly, "think of William. Or at least what we think's happened to him. You don't wanna go off in the woods by yourself at night — there might be a murderer out there."

"I don't want to hear about William or murderers. And I don't need your help."

For a long moment Denzil stared at her, then at last he nodded and stepped away.

"That inlet where you and Tawney were swimming — there's a path that forks. Take the left one. When that forks, go right. You can't miss it."

"Thanks."

She waited till she was out of sight before she started to run, and with Denzil's directions, found the house easily. Rattling the gate, she discovered it locked, but since there didn't seem to be any other way in, she hoisted herself over the top and landed clumsily on the other side.

Kate strained her ears through the deep night, surveying the house with apprehension. One light burned from a downstairs window; another window glowed on the second floor. *Is it really worth it? Can't it wait till tomorrow? Is this really important at all . . . ?*

She tapped with her flashlight on the door. The knock seemed to echo . . . on and on . . . back through empty rooms.

To her surprise, the door creaked slowly open.

"Hello?" Kate's voice was a whisper. "Is anyone here?"

Through dim light she could see a large hallway with doors opening off either side. At the end and straight ahead of her, a staircase rose up into half shadow.

"Gideon? Hello?"

For some reason Kate suddenly thought of William . . . the glove in Pet's mouth . . . the horrible thing inside it. . . .

She felt her feet moving her forward . . . up the stairs.

"Gideon?" Had she called out loud or was it only in her head? "Gideon, are you home?"

She thought she heard something . . . some soft, hidden movement . . . and saw a closed door with light seeping out underneath. She lifted her hand . . . curled her fingers around the knob. . . .

The groan went on forever, echoing down the hall as the door moved back on its hinges. Kate stood in the threshold, unable to believe what she was seeing.

It looked like a funeral parlor.

As her shocked eyes swept over the black-draped canopy bed to the black-skirted vanity table, she sagged weakly back against the wall. Everything in the room was black — bedspread, curtains, a pile of clothes dropped carelessly upon the floor, even the walls — and though the air was chilled and damp, an overpowering smell of dried flowers hung in the air.

Stunned, Kate's gaze went to the nightstand. A vase of dead roses stood beside a black velvet ribbon. A wreath of dead vines entwined with black streamers and black lace hung upon the wall. A sampler, cross-stitched with black thread, lay half finished upon a chair: *YEA, THOUGH I WALK THROUGH THE VALLEY OF THE SHADOW OF DEATH . . . death . . . death . . . death. . . .*

Kate didn't hear the footsteps move silently up the stairs.

Their stealthy approach behind her in the hall. . . .

Her cry of fear rang out as hands clamped onto her arms, pulling her back into the light.

"Kate! What are you doing here?"

As the grip slackened, Kate fell back against the wall, escape impossible.

"Gideon!"

There was no mistaking his total surprise — yet despite the intensity of his stare, he was pale and obviously shaken.

"What . . . what are you doing here, Kate? However did you find this place?"

"I'm sorry, Gideon, I know I shouldn't have come in, but — "

"This house is off-limits to everyone — guests included — "

"I'm . . . I'm sorry — only the door was open and I thought — " She thrust the watch out to him, her voice trembling. "Your watch. You dropped it back by the cave. I thought . . . you might need it."

There was a long silence. As Gideon's eyes dropped to her outstretched hand, he reached out slowly and took the watch.

"My . . . I didn't know, Kate . . . how kind of you . . . really. . . ."

As Kate's eyes narrowed in concern, Gideon

slipped the watch into his pocket, wandered to the top of the stairs, and turned to face her, as if he'd suddenly remembered she was there.

"Gideon, are you all right?"

He nodded, his voice polite but very thin. "Of course. Thank you for coming. I'll show you out now." His eyes flicked to the door behind her, where the black room lay beyond.

"Gideon," Kate said softly, "who's Rowena?"

And she didn't expect his hand to tremble so violently upon the bannister, clutching as if he would fall . . . and she wasn't prepared for the tears that slowly filled his eyes, though his face was calm and poised.

"Rowena," he whispered.

She started toward him, saw his eyes fix again on that door at the end of the hall.

"Rowena was my sister," he murmured. "She died a year ago."

Chapter 15

"Died?" Kate echoed. "But . . . but that's impossible. I don't understand. . . ."

Gideon didn't seem to hear, his eyes still fastened on that doorway behind them. "This watch is very special to me. I . . . thank you for bringing it. I'll walk you back."

"No, you don't have to," Kate said, but he was starting down the stairs. As she caught up with him, she reached out, covering one of his hands with her own. "Gideon, wait. There's something we have to talk about."

His eyes met hers, empty and sad. "I'm grateful, truly, but — "

"I've seen her, Gideon."

She saw his fingers tighten on the railing . . . a muscle clench in his jaw.

"Seen who? What are you talking about?"

"Rowena." Kate's voice dropped. In front of her, Gideon's head began a slow turn, but his body seemed frozen. "Rowena," she said again, nodding. "Or . . . at least . . . she said she was."

His eyes brimmed again. His hand gripped harder on the bannister. "Is this . . . some kind of joke?"

"Look at you," Kate mumbled. "Do you think I'd joke about something like this?"

He held her in an eternal stare, his head shaking at last. "No," he whispered. "No. Of course you wouldn't." He seemed to lose all strength then. Kate watched in alarm as he slid into a sitting position onto the stairs. "Tell me. Tell me what you saw."

Easing herself down beside him, she made a hesitant beginning. "Last night. I got lost and found your house by mistake. There was a girl outside the gates—she was dressed all in black—Gideon?"

He was shaking his head again, his cheeks paling. "*She* wore black. Always. She was fascinated with death — obsessed with it, really. You saw her room." It was an accusation, not a question, and Kate lowered her eyes. "She wrote about it. And all her paintings . . . her music . . . everything was about death. She was brilliant, you know. Brilliant."

Kate gave a lame nod. "Was she?"

"The most talented . . . the most beautiful. . . ." Something passed over his face, and he struggled for composure. "This girl you saw. She wore black — "

"Yes. A long skirt. Gloves. A veil. I couldn't see her face."

"But she spoke to you?"

Kate nodded. "It was weird . . . sort of threatening. She knew who I was . . . knew my name. She said someone — 'he' — had talked about me.

And . . . and she talked funny. Sometimes in rhyme."

His body stiffened, his hands gripping his knees. "Rhyme?" he said weakly.

"Yes. Like little songs almost."

"It was a game," he murmured. "A game we always played. Only she was the best at it. . . . she always had the best rhymes."

"But her voice . . ." Kate thought a moment, hearing it again in her mind. "I've heard people talk like that before . . . when their throats are raw . . . or their vocal cords are damaged. That's the sound she made. A funny sort of whisper."

"My God." Gideon's face twisted. "My God . . ." He stood up slowly, one hand reaching out to her in slow motion. "You really need to go now, Kate. Forgive me, but I have a lesson plan to finish, and it's been a tiring day."

"But — Gideon — "

"It was kind of you to bring the watch. I'd have been devastated to lose it — "

"But — "

"And I'm certain that whoever you saw last night was only out for some fun. I'm afraid you've been made the butt of a very tasteless joke — but that's what I'd expect from William's friends, and I assure you I'll speak to them about it."

To her dismay Kate suddenly found herself outside the gate, with Gideon releasing his grip on her arm. Before she could think of anything to say, he'd fastened the lock and strode back into the house, leaving her staring openmouthed.

Rowena . . . dead for a year!

Kate stood there, gazing through the bars, watching the dark, silent windows of the house. She could still feel the shock of Gideon's reaction — his nervousness — and something else. . . .

Fear.

With her thoughts in turmoil, Kate turned toward the path, and then screamed as someone stepped out of the darkness.

"Denzil!"

"So he threw you out, huh? Does this mean you're not teacher's pet anymore?"

Kate collapsed back against a tree, determined not to let him know how glad she was to see him. "You nearly gave me a heart attack!"

"And what did *he* give you? A heart*break*? Jeez, Kate, what's with you, anyway, just wandering into some guy's house?"

Kate stared at him. "You . . . you followed me."

"Yeah," Denzil grumbled. "So what if I did?" He shook his head impatiently. "You must be *loco*, snooping around like this! When I saw you go in, and then Gideon went in after you, I didn't know what to do."

"I thought he was home," Kate said weakly. "The door just opened by itself."

"Kate, what's going on?"

She stared at him a minute, then slowly let out a long sigh. "How'd you know?"

"How'd I *know*? It doesn't take a cleverly deductive mind — even though I *have* a cleverly deductive mind — to figure out something's weird when someone's bed gets knifed — "

"Okay, Denzil," Kate said seriously, "do you believe in ghosts?"

She took a deep breath and started in, trying to recount every strange incident from the day she'd arrived at camp. Denzil listened attentively, expression unchanged throughout the narration. When Kate was finally through, she shrugged and frowned.

"So. What do you think?"

"What do I think?" Denzil mused. He folded his arms across his chest and frowned back at her. "I think . . . jeez . . . I don't know *what* to think."

"You're a big help."

"But you're sure this girl called herself Rowena? You couldn't have misunderstood the name?"

Kate shook her head firmly. "When Gideon told me about William's weird friends, then I didn't worry about her anymore. It's obvious he doesn't like them — I just thought she wanted me to keep quiet so Gideon wouldn't know she'd been at the house."

"But *William* hasn't been there, right?"

"But that doesn't mean his friends couldn't still be hanging around. Maybe — " Kate thought a minute. "Maybe William isn't really missing at all. Maybe he just wants people to think he is."

"Yeah. And maybe Rowena really isn't dead."

They stared at each other uneasily.

"You *said* he practically ran you out of the house."

Kate looked doubtful. "I don't know. Maybe

that's just the way it seemed — like Gideon saying fear's in the mind of the beholder? Maybe he was just so upset hearing Rowena's name that he overreacted. I mean, *I* don't like people around me when I'm having trouble with painful memories."

Denzil groaned. "Will you stop sticking up for this guy?"

"Well, okay, since you know so much — where *is* Rowena?"

"Hey, I'm just coming up with theories here, I don't have to explain them." Denzil shone his flashlight over the thick trees, his face solemn. "But okay, try this. Say Rowena's possessive — for some Freudian reason — possessive of Gideon, maybe. So she sees him giving you all this special attention — "

"He doesn't give me special attention. I'm just one of the class."

"Yeah, right. You blew that excuse when I saw you go into his house tonight."

"Denzil, I told you, I took back the watch."

"I thought you were getting books." He grinned as she turned red and looked away. "And anyway, you were *jealous* of that watch. You wanted to pin him down about Rowena. I know the way your mind works. I saw that inscription."

Kate regarded his smug face and kept quiet.

"So maybe she's trying to scare you into staying away from Gideon. And things are getting a little out of hand."

"You mean, my clothes at the inlet, and my room and — "

"And the trap."

"What?"

"Kate, don't you hear *anything*? Pearce might have been right, what he said to you out there. That trap was set where *you* were supposed to be."

In a split second it all rushed back to her — Pearce walking out of the cave — the snap of metal jaws — the scream of agony —

"God. . . ." Kate clamped her arms around her chest, a fierce shiver going straight through her. "If Pearce hadn't been there — "

"Will you forget about Pearce?"

"Denzil, he probably saved my life!"

"Quit talking about him like he's some kind of hero! *He's* probably in on this Rowena thing, too."

"Okay, okay, but we still haven't figured out *why* they're hiding her."

"Hmmm . . ." He gave an exaggerated sigh. "Obsessed with death . . . dresses like a corpse . . . sacrifices small creatures in shower stalls. . . . I give up, Kate. Why *would* they wanna hide her?"

"Oh, Denzil, I — "

"Ssh! Someone's coming!"

In an instant, Kate found herself on her stomach in the weeds, her eyes focused through a tiny crack in the shrubbery. She heard the gate open and close . . . saw legs hurry past her hiding place. Scarcely daring to breathe, she felt Denzil nudging her from behind.

"Follow him," he hissed.

"Who?"

"Gideon. I wanna see what he's up to."

Feeling like a traitor, Kate held Denzil's arm as they tracked Gideon deeper and deeper into the woods. In the night silence where every sound was magnified, they had to keep a safe distance behind, Denzil aiming his flashlight slightly off the trail to avoid being seen. Gideon moved swiftly as if he'd been this way many times before, and more than once Kate thought they'd lost him. After what seemed like miles, she felt Denzil slow down and give her hand a cautious squeeze. Holding his finger to his lips, he squatted down and slowly parted a mass of leaves to peer out.

It was a cemetery. Spattered with moonlight, the tombstones shone gray . . . graves beneath dead leaves . . . dead weeds . . . everything . . . so dead . . . so final.

Gideon was standing beside one of the markers. Just standing there like some funerary statue carved from stone . . . his face hidden . . . staring down at the marker . . . at the black thing that fluttered there . . . the strange, wispy thing like some black dying bird, just flowing there, beckoning, as Gideon reached out . . . reached down. . . .

"No!" His cry echoed through the night . . . caught in the trees . . . flung back again . . . again. . . .

"Denzil!" a voice called. "Denzil? Where *are* you!"

Paralyzed, Kate recognized Tawney's voice through the trees. As she and Denzil exchanged horrified looks, Gideon turned and raced past them, swallowed immediately by the night.

"C'mon!" Denzil jumped up and flung his flashlight beam onto the spot where Gideon had been standing. The black, fluttering thing was gone. "Damn, damn, *damn*!"

"Denzil?" Tawney yelled again. "I *saw* you heading for the woods! Come on out — you have a *phone* call! If you're trying to scare me, it won't work!"

"Don't answer her," Denzil said. "Maybe she'll wander away, and we'll never see her again."

"Denzil, stop it," Kate said, but he was moving forward, exploring the cemetery with his flashlight, the pale glow skipping over that one grave, over that name on the stone, shaking, like his hands were shaking —

ROWENA DREWE
BELOVED —

Kate jerked him away, her voice angry and panicky. "Now are you satisfied? She's dead! She's here, and she's — "

"What *was* that?" Denzil shone the light in her eyes, and she put up one arm to ward it off. "What was that thing he was looking at?"

"I don't know." Kate was backing away, suddenly unable to bear this place a moment longer. "A scarf or something, I — "

"Kate, take a look at this."

She saw him untangle something from a low-sweeping branch and hold it into the light.

"It's some kind of black material. He must have torn it, trying to get it loose. And you're right, see? It's kind of gauzy like a scarf — "

"Or a veil." Kate reached out with trembling fingers and took the cloth from him. "It could be a veil . . . like Rowena was wearing . . . and . . ."

As her voice trailed off, Denzil moved closer, adding his light to hers. "Kate, what's wrong?"

"The smell," she mumbled. "Don't you recognize it?"

And as he sniffed the air, she held the material beneath his nose, drawing it back again, inhaling deeply.

"What are you talking about?"

"I've smelled it before," Kate said flatly. "Upstairs in Gideon's house. Like dead flowers."

"So? It's fall, remember? Everything's dying."

"And somewhere else." She was silent a moment as her eyes focused wide on his face. "My room, Denzil," she murmured. "That funny smell in my cabin . . . mixed with the smell of blood."

Chapter 16

"Are you sure?" Denzil frowned. "About that smell, I mean?" Back in Kate's cabin, he stretched out on her bed and propped his chin on folded arms. Kate, sitting beside him, straightened her back against the wall and nodded.

"It's a strange smell . . . almost suffocating. I couldn't quite place it in Rowena's room, but I knew I'd smelled it before." She thought a moment. "Should we go to the police?"

Denzil's laugh burst out before he could stop it. "And tell them *what*?"

"Well, that some *dead* girl's after me might be a good place to start." Kate looked injured.

"We don't have a bit of proof. As a matter of fact, there's not a whole lot of stuff we know *anything* about."

"Do you think he heard us following him?" Kate sounded worried as Denzil shrugged.

"Maybe. You're the only one who has a chance to find out anything. Start asking him about his family and stuff."

"I can't do that."

"Sure you can. You're the teacher's pet, remember? He *likes* you. He just might let something slip about William and Rowena."

From the other bed, Tawney lifted a questioning finger. "Now . . . one more time . . . what exactly's going on?"

Denzil flopped back down with a groan. "You never shoulda told her. Not any of it."

"I want her to know." Kate cast Tawney a thin smile. "I need her moral support."

"You're just afraid I'll screw something up," Tawney sighed. "But I *can't* screw it up if I don't understand it to begin with."

"Trust me," Denzil forced a smile. "It's what you do best." He yawned and glanced at Kate. "You gonna be okay here tonight? Wanna stay with Tawney? Want *me* to stay with you?"

In spite of everything, Kate smiled, reaching down to hug him. "Thanks, but I don't think I'll have any trouble sleeping. Do you need to go to the village tomorrow?"

"Oh, here it comes, I knew it. Poor Pearce. You simply *must* go and check on poor Pearce."

"Miss Bunceton," Kate corrected him. "Do I get a ride or not?"

"Sure. But I still don't think you should sleep alone."

"I told you, I'll be perfectly fine. Good night."

Kate watched her friends leave and locked up behind them, but lying in bed afterwards she wished she'd let them stay. She couldn't control the pictures whirling through her head — *William . . . Rowena . . . Gideon . . . Pearce. . . .* The night was full of secrets. And she had an unshakable feeling that something awful was about to happen.

At long last she drifted off, tossing and turning in fitful sleep. When she bolted up in bed, gasping, she looked around the darkened room in confusion, wondering what had woken her. Silence crushed in, yet just beneath it she was sure she'd heard something oddly out of place in the night.

Her eyes swung to the door, half expecting the knob to turn.

Everything was still.

Inching up on her knees, she caught hold of the curtains above her bed. Her ears strained through the quiet, her heart pounding in her throat. She tasted the sharp tang of fear and tried to choke it back.

Slowly . . . slowly . . . she pulled the curtains apart. . . .

And stared into someone's face.

Even in the dark the eyes were wide and gleaming, the gaze fixed on hers as if they'd known the exact spot, the exact moment she'd peer out.

With a shriek Kate let the curtains fall, leaping from her bed, huddling in the corner, screaming . . . screaming. . . .

She didn't know how long she screamed.

Only when her voice gave out, when her strength gave out . . . when she realized nothing else was going to happen, did a surge of anger replace her fear, flinging her back onto her bed, tearing at the curtains —

No one was there.

In the shifting shadows there was only the endless black night and all its mysterious whispers she couldn't recognize. . . .

But she had recognized something.

And now, collapsing back onto her pillow, she saw those eyes again, wide and staring in her mind . . . the strange, wild expression masking their gentleness. . . .

"Gideon," she whispered. "Gideon . . . why?"

"Are you positive?" Denzil asked again, scuffing his feet along the path. "I mean, are you absolutely — ?"

"Well, how can I be absolutely sure?" Kate's voice raised, her shoulders shrugging helplessly. "It was dark and scary — but, yes, I'm *almost* positive it was Gideon."

"You're not staying alone tonight, understand? Me or Tawney, take your pick."

"It isn't really like he *did* anything," Kate rambled on, more to herself than to Denzil. "He was just *there*. It's not like he tried to get in or — "

"Or what? Come on, let's make up something really gruesome."

Kate glanced at him, but Denzil wasn't smiling. "I shouldn't have told you. Now you're upset."

"Upset?" Denzil hooked his thumbs in his pants and gave a swagger. "Nah, I'm not upset. I think it's fun when people I care about are being scared out of their minds. It makes life interesting."

"Denzil — "

"I mean it, Kate. Till we find out what's going on around here, I don't think you should stay by yourself." He nodded for emphasis, then cast her an almost hopeful look. "You're *positive* you weren't dreaming?"

"I wasn't dreaming. And don't tell Tawney. If I stay with her, I don't want her to be scared."

"Well, I'm scared." Denzil stopped, shading his eyes from the sun. "There's the kitchen and there's Tawney outside — which means she did something — which *always* scares me."

As they neared the back door, Tawney was standing out on the steps, her hands on her hips, looking totally bewildered.

"So *there* you are!" she burst out. "I looked and *looked* for you, and nobody knew where you were! I had to make muffins all by myself, and they burned, and the fire alarm went off, and we all had to leave the building." She paused, her huge eyes going even wider. "And now they won't let me back in."

"Oh, Tawney," Kate sympathized, trying to hide a smile, "I'm so sorry. Was it really that bad?"

"*I* didn't think so, but everyone else got upset about it. And Gideon came by looking for you, Kate, and — "

"Gideon? For me?" Kate exchanged looks with Denzil. "What did he want?"

"I just don't know," Tawney shook her head.

"But they won't let me back in the kitchen now, so I don't know what I'm supposed to do."

"Come on," Denzil said, flinging an arm around her shoulders. "You can help me."

"They say I need a supervisor," Tawney went on. "They say I'm a real case."

"You're just very innovative," Denzil soothed, winking back at Kate over his shoulder. "Don't they appreciate talent when they see it in action?"

"And since I had to stay out here," Tawney said defensively, "I wrote a poem about it. It's called 'Muffin Madness, My Early Morning Sadness.' "

"Please — " Denzil held up a hand. "Read it to me later. After I've eaten. You know how — emotional — your poems always make me feel."

"Well, I try to put so much feeling into them. . . ."

"You certainly do." Denzil paused in the kitchen door and motioned to Kate. "Hey, what about some grub?"

"Maybe I should try to find Gideon first."

"Oh, but he's not here." Tawney looked back, shaking her head. "He took Pearce's truck and drove off somewhere."

"Come on," Denzil insisted. "After breakfast we'll go for a ride, and you can visit Miss B."

Obligingly Kate followed them in, but it was hard to concentrate on food. She scarcely heard the bustle around her in the kitchen and jumped, startled, as Denzil took her arm.

"Earth to Kate. Come in, please."

"Sorry." Kate gave a rueful smile. "I guess my

mind's on other things. What did you say?"

"I said, that horror hunt tomorrow night should be fun." He looked at her a minute, then sighed. "Horror hunt. *¿Comprendes, amiga?*"

"Oh. Right." Kate's attention struggled back. "I saw it in the brochure, but I wasn't sure what it was."

"Like a scavenger hunt. Only we hunt for horrors and terrible, scary things. You know, like rats . . . and spiders . . . and Pearce."

"Well, that's not very hard." Tawney frowned. "We already know where to find Pearce."

Denzil faced her, all seriousness. "How do you catch a zombie?"

"I don't know. How?"

"In a zombie trap. Oops, too late. Someone already beat us to it."

Kate gave him a withering look. "You are one sick person."

"Thanks." Denzil grinned. "Shall we go?"

Kate was glad when Denzil and Tawney let her out at the clinic, promising to pick her up again in an hour. It was getting harder and harder for her to focus on what was going on around her, and the stark, sterile atmosphere of the clinic was a welcome relief. When she peeked in at Miss Bunceton's door, her teacher was propped up in bed watching a soap opera.

"Kate! How lovely to see you!" Miss Bunceton managed to get the greeting out despite her swollen face. "Well, honestly, can you imagine such a thing as this! Who would ever have thought I'd be so *allergic* to some wretched plant! That'll teach me to have my passionate hero woo my heroine on a bed of pretty green ivy in the woods!"

Kate laughed, relieved. It was good to see her teacher again. Somehow it put everything into a sane, proper perspective.

"Having a good time, I trust?" Miss Bunceton went on. "Learning a lot? Enjoying yourself?"

Fun . . . I was here to have a good time. . . . Kate blinked, startled. She'd almost forgotten about the fun part.

"Well, I love Gideon's class. And we're going on a horror hunt tomorrow night." She forced brightness into her voice. "There never seems to be a dull moment."

"Splendid! I feel ghastly for abandoning you like this. I'm a circus sideshow, my dear, just look at the size of me!"

Kate chuckled. "Do you know how long you'll have to stay? I can bring some more of your things, or if there's something you need — books — food — "

"How sweet of you, but don't trouble yourself. Good heavens, I'm going to try and get some rest today if I can — I certainly didn't get any last night! You remember that *ill*-tempered Pearce fellow who picked us up the other day? Well, he came in with some emergency, and they put him in the room next door. Good heavens, he moaned and groaned all night — talking out of his head — nightmares or whatever, I'm sure I don't know, but I didn't get a *wink* of sleep."

"Well . . ." Kate's heart sank, imagining his pain, "maybe the nurse can give you something to help you sleep tonight."

"They should give *him* something," Miss Bunceton retorted. "Like a gag . . . or a transfer to a soundproof room!"

The time passed cheerfully. Promising to keep in touch, Kate said good-bye, then stood out in the hall, staring at the next door down. There was no telling what kind of mood Pearce might be in after a restless night . . . still, what he'd been through was too horrible to ignore. She approached the door cautiously, part of her wanting to turn back. *You're a hypocrite, Kate Rawlins, you're not just worried about Pearce, you're wondering if he'll remember that moment you shared . . . the kisses . . . that tenderness so unlike him.*

She started to knock . . . heard familiar voices inside . . . and dropped her arm back to her side.

The door was partway open. From where she stood, she had a clear view of the hospital bed without being seen. Pearce still looked pale. Gideon, in a chair beside him, leaned forward, his face drawn and troubled.

"I know it can't be true," he said slowly. "I know . . . it's impossible . . . but it just doesn't make any sense."

Pearce's head moved slightly against the pillows. "It's got to be one of William's friends — you remember that girl, especially. I can't remember her name — she's always doing weird things to get his attention."

"But that's something else," Gideon said, shaking his head. "Where *is* William?"

"Gideon, this isn't anything new. He's done this hundreds of times before."

"But this time is different," Gideon insisted.

"How?"

"I . . . I don't know. I just . . . feel it." Gideon stared at a spot on the wall. "Yesterday when you called me away from Kate because you'd found William's jacket by the lake . . . and then . . . that thing with his glove — "

Pearce moaned, whether from pain or exasperation, Kate couldn't tell. "You know he's just on a binge somewhere. You know he's just lost his gloves, that's all. He wouldn't remember his own head if it wasn't attached, you *know* that."

"Yes . . . yes, I know." Gideon stood and began pacing, hands in his pockets, head down. "Pearce . . . I . . . I know it's painful to talk about. . . ."

Pearce stared at him for several moments. Even from where Kate stood she could see his eyes darkening with sadness. "Please, Gideon," he whispered at last. "Please don't do this to me."

"Just tell me again." Gideon stopped and faced him. "Just tell me again that she's dead."

Slowly Pearce's head dropped back, his cheeks going whiter, his eyes closing. One hand brushed at his forehead, as if trying to catch an elusive memory. "Gideon . . ."

"It's just that I can't stop thinking about it — even after all this time — how she was alone and none of us were with her — "

"Stop." Pearce's head moved back and forth upon the pillow. "I don't want to hear this again — "

"None of us were with her, and I can't get it out of my mind! And all that time I had to think about things — after I had that breakdown — all that time, trying to get better, trying to forget — but I *can't*! She was so beautiful, and she loved us so much — and she died like that — trapped — and no one to help her — "

Tears squeezed from the corners of Pearce's eyes. "Don't! I can't think about it anymore — please!"

"And now Kate says she *saw* her! Do you hear me, Pearce? She saw *Rowena* — dressed in black, talking in rhymes, outside the gates, for Christ's sake!"

"Gideon — "

"The girl said her name — said *Rowena* — my God, Pearce, outside the gates — was she trying to get *in*?" He stood there, arms out in appeal, and Pearce lay still, only the sound of his choked breathing disturbing the painful silence. "Pearce," Gideon murmured at last, "Pearce, I'm sorry . . . I'm . . ."

Pearce drew a shaky breath. "Why are you doing this? You know what happened. You've seen the grave."

A shudder went through Gideon as he stood there. "I know what I was *told*. But I wasn't there. I wasn't at the funeral . . . and neither was William."

Pearce's eyes slowly focused on Gideon's face. "William couldn't come because of his burns. They wouldn't let him out of the hospital. And you . . ."

He left the sentence unfinished, and Gideon threw him a guilty look.

"I know. I fell apart. I wasn't any use to you when you needed me."

"Well, what did you expect me to do?" Pearce whispered. "I couldn't just wait for you. I had to bury her."

Gideon crossed to the window and looked out, his face creased with suffering. "Kate said the girl's voice sounded as if her vocal cords had been damaged. If a person were burned badly enough in a fire — "

"Christ, Gideon!" Pearce struggled to sit straight, a wave of pain making him gasp. "Why don't you just dig up the damn grave? Just go home and get a shovel and — "

"William is *missing*!" Gideon's hands slammed down on the windowsill. "She was trying to kill William that night — *you* know it, and *I* know it — "

"So now her ghost is back to finish the job?"

"Look. Look what I found. Last night. I went to the cemetery and — "

"Oh, Gideon, why — "

"Just *look* at it! *Her* scarf!"

"A piece of material! What does that prove? It could be anyone's!"

Gideon pushed it into his face. "*Smell* it!"

"It smells like the woods smell . . . like everything around camp smells this time of year — "

"It's *her* smell, you know it is! *Her* perfume! The flowers in *her* room! And it was on *her* tombstone!"

Pearce fell back once more, gripping the sides of his head. "Gideon, don't put yourself through this — *please* — don't put *me* through it! You couldn't deal with it last time, you were seeing her in every crowd, in every shadow, she was talking to you in your *dreams*, for Christ's sake — don't dredge it all up again!" His voice had risen, pleading, but now it sank again, barely a whisper. "Please, Gideon . . . please. . . ."

As Kate watched through tears, Gideon leaned down and hugged Pearce, then turned, and started for the door.

"Where are you going?" Pearce demanded.

"Home. I'm sorry. Forget about all this. Try and rest."

"Wait — what are you going to do?" Pearce tried to scoot to the side of the bed as if he would follow, but his pain stopped him. "Gideon? I'm coming home, do you hear me? I won't stay in this stupid — Gideon, will you stop? Damn!" He hit the bed as hard as he could, then let out a groan.

Kate didn't have time to hide. Gideon was upon her so quickly that all she could do was stare at him and try to stammer an explanation.

"Kate." Gideon stopped, his body going rigid. "I didn't hear you knock."

"Oh, Gideon, hi!" she said, knowing how forced her cheerfulness sounded, how phony, and *yes, those are the eyes, the ones that watched in my window last night, that strange look of — what?* "I . . . that is . . . I just got here. This very second, in fact. I just came to see how Pearce is doing."

"Excuse me." Gideon shoved past her, and as she cast a despairing look at Pearce, he sank back with a sigh.

"Let him go."

"But look at him — he's so upset — "

"You don't understand. You . . ." Pearce shook his head, his eyes closing wearily. "Just . . . stay away from him. And from me."

Chapter 17

For a long moment Kate couldn't believe what she was hearing. *But you kissed me — don't you remember? — and I stayed with you and kept you safe and told you everything would be all right.* . . . His indifference hurt her now, but she tried to sound casual.

"How are you feeling?"

"How long have you been there?" His look was so intense that a lie stuck in her throat. "I thought so." He nodded.

Kate hung her head and leaned against the door frame. "I didn't mean to eavesdrop. I was visiting Miss Bunceton next door and I — really — wanted to see how you were."

"Couldn't be better."

"I was worried about you," Kate said in a small voice.

He cast her a sidelong glance, then fixed his eyes on the window. "It's not as bad as they thought. I'll just be laid up for a while."

"That's good. You should rest."

"I can't. I'm worried about Gideon. I have to get home."

"It's probably everything . . . William and the conference . . . all the pressure."

"No," Pearce said softly. "No. It's . . . something else. It's . . ." He lapsed into silence, and Kate took a cautious step toward his bed.

"Pearce . . . tell me about Rowena."

There was no surprise on his face when she said it. There was nothing at all. He stared out at the autumn afternoon, and his face was as still as stone.

"She was beautiful," he said. "She was . . ." A humorless laugh sounded in his throat. "Unusual."

"Were she and Gideon very close?"

"Inseparable." His eyes shifted onto her puzzled face. "Closer than anyone could guess."

Kate nodded slowly. "It's very sad, isn't it."

"He went to pieces when she died. He still hasn't gotten over it." A thoughtful silence, then, "I don't think he ever will."

An unexpected coldness crept over her. She rubbed her arms and said, "I didn't imagine what I saw. I told Gideon the truth. The girl *did* say her name was Rowena."

"I'm not surprised," Pearce said without hesitation. "William's friends will do anything for effect. But I'm afraid it's stirred up all the old emotions in Gideon again."

"I'm so sorry. If I'd known, I'd never have mentioned it."

He gave a vague nod and looked as if he believed

her. "I think he still blames himself because he wasn't here when she died. Like maybe he could have stopped it. But it was better for him to be away. Some people hold on too tight to those they love. They never want anything to change."

"Are you talking about Gideon?"

"No. Rowena."

"What did she look like?"

"Light brown hair . . . strange-colored eyes. A lot like Gideon's, actually. She looked a lot like Gideon."

The eyes . . . at my window . . . Rowena? Not Gideon but Rowena? "And what . . . what happened to her?"

His head moved slowly upon the pillow. "Just stay away from him. You can't help him. It's too . . ." His voice faded, and Kate was beside his bed, reaching gently for his arm.

"But I'd like to help him, if I can."

"You can't. All you can do is stay away. From both of us."

"I . . . I don't understand — "

"Gideon really likes you," Pearce said huskily. "I can see it." He thought a moment, then added, "Rowena would be jealous of that."

Part of her wrestled with instant fear; part of her with confusion. "Last night . . . I guess you were in shock. There's probably a lot you don't remember." Turning for the door, his voice stopped her.

"I remember," he said quietly.

She froze, one hand upon the door. When she

turned and faced him again, he looked uncomfortable and averted his eyes.

"You know," she said softly, "I don't think you're nearly as scary as you'd like people to think you are."

He seemed to mull the words over. The faintest hint of a smile struggled over his lips, and he allowed her a quick glance, almost shy. "Maybe," he mumbled grudgingly.

"I'll come back to see you," she promised.

"At home. I'm not staying."

"Well . . . we'll see."

Kate was still puzzling over Pearce's words when she got back to camp, though she'd kept up a valiant effort all the way home to act as if nothing were wrong. The more she learned about Rowena, the more apprehensive she felt . . . the more *alive* the girl became . . . the more possible the whole thing seemed. Yet deep down Kate knew it *wasn't* possible, that Rowena had died in a fire, and that whatever was going on was something strange and dangerous that she couldn't understand. Stay away from Gideon, Pearce had said — but why? Because of his nervous breakdown? Did Pearce think he was unstable? *Or could it be that Pearce is . . . jealous?* And stay away from me, Pearce had said, Gideon really likes you. *Is it that Pearce doesn't want to compete with Gideon?* And then Pearce's other words kept drifting back — "Rowena would be jealous of that." *But Rowena's dead . . . she can't be jealous of me . . . she's dead . . . she died in a fire. . . .*

"Denzil?" Kate caught hold of his arm as he jumped out of the van. "I need to ask you something."

"What took you so long?" He grinned. "Of course I'll marry you."

Kate ignored him, her voice urgent. "You remember that girl you told me about — Merriam — the one last summer?"

"Who threw herself all over Gideon? Yeah. What about her?"

"How did she die?"

Denzil cocked his head at her, eyes narrowing. "Is this really necessary?"

"Yes. I want to know."

"Okay," he sighed. "It was a fire. She died in a fire."

Kate's skin crawled. "A . . . fire? But you said — I thought — it was suicide — "

"Right. Deliberately set. She waited till she was alone and — come on, do I have to go into all the gory details? She started it in her room at her house and that was that. Why? What's the big deal?"

"It's . . . for this story I'm thinking of," Kate mumbled.

"Great. Remember to cut me in for royalties."

Kate nodded and backed away. "I have to go to class."

"Mind taking notes for me again?" His grin faltered and went crooked. "You okay?"

Kate smiled. "Yeah, see you later."

There was a notice on the door that Gideon's class had been canceled. With the scene at the clinic still haunting her, Kate set out walking, hoping to distract her growing uneasiness. Sitting by the lake, trying to make herself at one with its deep serenity, she supposed she'd heard the sound in the woods for some time before it actually registered. When she followed it to an overgrown thicket, she was surprised to see Gideon there, his jeans and shirt soaked with sweat, an axe poised above his head as he stood back and surveyed the tree he was cutting. She stood for a long time, staring at the axe, remembering the shadow on the bank of the inlet. She sensed somehow that Gideon knew she was there, though he went doggedly back to the tree again, breaking limbs with his bare hands, flinging them roughly to the growing pile at his feet. At last the axe lowered. He wiped at his upper lip and afforded her a quick glance.

"I'm sorry about class. I know people were counting on me."

"I don't think they'll mind," Kate said quietly. "I heard they were all going horseback riding somewhere."

"Then why aren't you with them?"

"I'd rather be here with you."

Another glance, and his hand rested lightly on his hip. "You must be desperate for entertainment, if this is the best you can do."

Kate ignored him. "Is this more fun for you than teaching?"

"Pearce isn't here. Someone has to do his work."

"Don't you have employees for this sort of thing? I'm sure if you just asked someone — "

"It's good for me." Gideon cut her off. "I feel better afterwards." He picked up the axe again, turning it over slowly in his hands. "The control one has . . ." For a moment he stared at it, then his eyes slid over her and stayed.

"Pearce looks good — " Kate changed the subject — "don't you think so?"

He nodded, rather mechanically, Kate noted.

"He wants to come home," she said.

"Tomorrow, perhaps. By tomorrow they'll be begging me to take him." He gave a wry smile. "So. What do you expect me to say?"

Kate looked surprised. "I don't expect you to say anything."

"You didn't come just to chat. Pearce talked about me, didn't he? About my . . . condition? My credibility?"

Kate saw the muscle tense in his jaw, the spots of color on his cheeks. His hand tightened around the axe handle and he swung so hard that she jumped.

"He didn't say much at all. Gideon — " Kate bit her lip, almost afraid to go on. "Gideon, if there's anything you want to talk about — anything at all — I *want* to hear it. I want to."

"Don't feel sorry for me. Nothing makes me angrier." Another blow with the axe, and the tree shook to its very roots.

"I'm not feeling sorry for you. I'm just trying to make some sense of everything. William's friends don't know me, and they don't have any reason to come after me, even if they *did* know me. But *someone* wants to scare me, and I want to know who and why."

He struck another blow. The blade wedged in the fleshy part of the tree, and he worked it out . . . twisting it . . . side to side. "I thought you liked to be scared."

Something about the way he said it . . . the dark amusement she couldn't quite read. Kate stared at him, and then the words blurted out before she could stop them.

"And I thought you liked me. So why won't you help?"

This time the axe froze in midair . . . quivered . . . lowered slowly to the ground.

"I do like you," he said hoarsely. "And that's why this frightens me more than you could ever know." As she gazed up at him, he gave a sigh and came to stand beside her. "It's not just Rowena. It's William. It's . . . everything. Everything is very, very . . . wrong, somehow."

"You're worried about William, aren't you? You don't think he's just hidden himself off somewhere."

"No. I think he's dead."

Kate's eyes widened. Gideon leaned back against a tree and looked down at her.

"He could have had so much — William — but he's always been jealous of everyone and everything. He's the most pathetic person I've ever known. He hated Rowena for her beauty, and me for my talent. As long as I can remember, he's begrudged us every happiness and every accomplishment. He spoils anything pure and good. He can't bear to see anyone else happy."

"And he's always been like that? Even when your parents were alive?"

"Yes. They tried very hard to deal with it, but nothing seemed to work. He always won them over with promises to reform."

"Which he always broke?"

Gideon nodded. "He's always hated Pearce, felt that Pearce is beneath him. William took great pleasure in humiliating him, and he was jealous of Pearce and Rowena's relationship. Rowena adored Pearce — not as her adopted brother; it was always more than that. They were in love. And Rowena was always afraid of William, ever since she was a child. God only knows what he did to torment her when no one was looking — I'm sure he threatened her with horrible things, but she'd never talk about him."

"But that's so awful." Kate shook her head. "So terrible for all of you, what he's put you through — "

"After the accident, there were only the four of us. Rowena was inconsolable, and even though she and I had always been very close, she seemed to need me so much more after that. She . . . well . . . *clung* to me . . . depended on me far too much. I should never have allowed her to grow that dependent . . . but I felt sorry for her and wanted to help."

"Because you were her security," Kate thought

aloud. "Her protection from William."

"Yes, I tried to protect her from William. I kept *trying* to get him to leave, but he wouldn't. He was drinking and running up hundreds of bills we couldn't pay. Pearce found work in the village to help out, but I had to find what jobs I could in other towns nearby. I hated it, going off and leaving her, but at least I knew Pearce was watching out for her. And then I found out William was trying to get rid of Pearce — trying to drive him off the property, making life miserable for him — even more than usual. Pearce wouldn't leave without Rowena. And William wouldn't let Rowena leave."

"Couldn't they just sneak away? Without William knowing?"

"They tried. Once. But somehow William found out about it and did something to their car. Pearce was in a coma for days. Rowena . . . withdrew even more."

"But surely there was some kind of legal action — "

Gideon shook his head miserably. "William had lawyer friends, as well — and as crooked as they come. I even made a deal with him — I'd already gotten some favorable comments about one of my manuscripts, a publisher who was definitely interested — so I told William I'd put *his* name on it if he'd just take the royalties and leave."

"But he didn't go?"

Gideon ran one hand through his hair and closed his eyes. "I should have known better, but I would have tried *anything*. And William *loved* the sudden notice the book brought him. He started playing the part of the famous author, passing himself off as some great literary genius. It was his idea to start having writers conferences here, and I agreed because we needed the money so badly."

Kate looked down at the windblown leaves and tried to shut out the pain in Gideon's voice.

"And then" — he drew a shaky breath — "that night. Pearce was on a job and was spending the night in the village. And I . . . was two hundred miles away. They knocked on his door about midnight . . . said there was a fire up at the house — " Gideon closed his eyes and was silent. After a moment he spoke again, chillingly calm. "By the time I got there, it was over. We think Rowena set the fire deliberately — to kill William — but somehow . . . she got trapped. Pearce tried to go in after her, but the heat and smoke were too much for him. They kept him at the clinic overnight. William was rushed to the main hospital. There was . . . nothing left of Rowena."

Kate swallowed over the lump in her throat, forcing horrible images from her mind. "Gideon — "

"I *had* to work, we *needed* the money — "

"Of course you did! You were doing the right thing. You were helping her — "

"But if only I'd been there! Maybe it wouldn't have happened — or maybe I could have saved her — "

"You can't keep thinking that. You can't keep blaming yourself." Yet Kate knew by the desperation in his voice that her words had no effect; the guilt had been there too long. "Gideon, please — don't do this. You're hurting yourself so much, and it won't change what happened."

"I fell apart," he said, as if she hadn't spoken. "I completely fell apart. I couldn't deal with it. I still can't."

"Please stop — I'm telling you, all this talk won't change things — "

"But what if things *are* changed?" Gideon said slowly, and his eyes burned into her with such sudden darkness . . . such sudden emptiness. "What if things have *always* been changed?"

"What — what are you — ?"

"I never saw the remains. I didn't, and William didn't. What if . . . Rowena is still alive?"

Kate felt her head move . . . someone else's head on someone else's shoulders. "Gideon . . ."

"And it *was* her outside the house, and she *did* tell you her name, and William is missing because she finally succeeded in doing what she wanted to do her whole life — "

"But — but — " Kate's mind was spinning out of control. "Where would she live? *How* would she live?"

"And maybe she's not buried at all, she just set the fire and disappeared, and now she's having her revenge — " He came closer. "You think I'm crazy, I know. Poor Gideon, never quite recovered from the shock — but *you're* the one who said it couldn't be William's friends, didn't you? You're the one — "

"I'm the one being *terrorized*! There was blood

in my room — my things practically destroyed — someone slashed up my clothes — and *why* did that trap just happen to be there at that cave you sent me to?" She hadn't realized her voice was getting louder or that she'd leaped to her feet or that her face was inches from his as all her anger and fear spewed out. She didn't even realize his arms were around her until she felt his kisses smothering her cries and felt warm tears streaking her cheeks. "Oh, Gideon," she sobbed, "if it's really Rowena, why does she want to hurt *me*?"

For an endless moment there were only Kate's quiet tears and Gideon's comforting sounds as he held her.

"My God, Kate, my God. . . ." He sounded dazed, pulling away from her, his expression alarmed. "Just listen to me — to *us*! You must think me completely mad — carrying on the way I have, frightening you like this — frightening *myself*! Of course Rowena's not alive — it's absolutely impossible — ridiculous to even consider. I don't know what's gotten into me — William disappearing the way he has, and the power of suggestion, I suppose — for God's sake, Kate, can you forgive me? Of course there's no one after you, it's only pranks — some other student's envy because you're the most talented writer in the lot. And that trap — Pearce will tell you about our problems with poachers. It's nothing new, believe me. The trap was meant for no one . . . only some defenseless animal."

Kate looked up at him, wanting so much to believe him. "Why do you think William's dead?"

Gideon hesitated, looked as though he were debating over his answer. "It's . . . just a feeling."

"It's the glove," Kate said accusingly. "The one I found on our walk. It *was* his, wasn't it?"

"All right, so it *was*. But he's always losing his gloves, that's nothing suspicious."

"You turned pale when you saw it," Kate challenged him. "And now you're lying to me."

Gideon's sigh was tinged with impatience. "Let's walk back. It must be time for dinner."

"I can find my own way, thank you very much."

"Kate! Come back — don't be like that."

But Kate didn't turn around nor did she stop walking until she saw the lodge ahead and Tawney waving at her from the porch.

"Kate! Did you know you have a message in here?"

Puzzled, Kate followed her inside and stared at the envelope that was tacked to the bulletin board on the wall.

"I don't know how long it's been there." Tawney shrugged apologetically. "I hardly ever come in here, and there's always so much junk on this board anyway. One of the other girls noticed it, so I thought I'd better tell you."

"Thanks, Tawney," Kate mumbled. She stared at her name typed on the envelope. "I can't imagine . . ."

"Oh, I hope it's not bad news," Tawney worried. "But they wouldn't just stick it up there, would they? Wouldn't they send a telegram or a messenger or a private detective or something?"

Kate gave a wry smile. "Let's have a look."

She pulled the paper out and unfolded it.

She read the four neat lines in the middle of the page.

She felt the room recede around her . . . sway . . . and fade into a black, deep shadow.

"Kate?" Tawney whispered. "What is it?"

With shaking fingers, Kate handed over the paper, but the typed words flashed like neon in her brain.

One little teacher's pet
Feeling so perplexed . . .
William's gone to pieces
And you'll . . . be . . . next.

Chapter 18

"Anybody could've put it there," said Denzil. "People go in and out all day and night. Besides, we don't even know how long it was up before somebody noticed it."

"So it could have been put there yesterday," Kate figured.

"Yeah, or any other time. Did you notice anyone watching when you read it?"

Kate shook her head. "I was too upset to notice. We came straight here."

Beside her, Tawney was wringing her hands, her eyes growing wide with fear. "Oh, what does that *mean* about William going to pieces! It has something to do with that hand Kate thought she saw, doesn't it, and you're just not telling me — "

Denzil threw a look at Kate. "Don't worry about it. It's just somebody playing a joke."

"Oh, I'm so scared! There might be pieces of William all over camp, and we'll never know where we'll *trip* over him or *fall* over him or — "

"Tawney." Denzil grabbed her and glared as several of the kitchen crew tossed curious glances their way. "Will you please . . . shut . . . up? What are you trying to do, anyway? Start a stampede? We don't want everyone getting spooked about this — we're not even sure what's going on!"

Tawney nodded vigorously, and Denzil sighed, turning his attention back to a sinkful of pots and pans.

"I told you," he grumbled. "I told you not to trust Gideon."

"Not trust Gideon!" Kate burst out. "How can you say that? After all the *pain* he's been through — the *grief* — the — "

"And has it ever occurred to you," Denzil said calmly, "that he might be a little off balance?" He tapped his head. "The whole family, as a matter of fact. All of them *loco*."

Kate bristled. "I can't even believe you're thinking such a thing! I wish now I hadn't even told you what he said! He trusted me!"

"He caught you," Denzil cut in. "You're bound to him now. He revealed deep, dark secrets to you." Denzil snorted. "Just another reason for someone to want you out of the way."

"And what is *that* supposed to mean?"

"Look, the closer you get to this guy, the more dangerous it seems to be getting for you. Or haven't you noticed? How do you even know Gideon's telling the truth?"

"Well, why *wouldn't* he be telling me the truth?" she asked indignantly.

"Because he's a writer. He tells stories. He *manipulates* people, remember?"

"But this isn't his new novel," Tawney spoke up solemnly. "This is real-life horror."

"How do you know? Maybe he's testing out a new *plot*. Maybe Rowena is really his *wife*, huh? Did you ever think of that?"

"Ooh." Tawney shivered. "I never did! *That's* even scarier!"

"For all you know," Denzil faced Kate in disgust, "Rowena might be his worst childhood nightmare."

The three fell silent, a strange coldness between them.

"Well, come on," Denzil insisted, "the guy had a *breakdown*. There's something missing upstairs, and you have to admit — "

"Denzil, I don't want to hear any more of this," Kate said angrily. "You and I both saw the grave. And Pearce talked about Rowena, too — "

"We saw a stone with a name on it. Christ, Pearce might be *humoring* Gideon just 'cause he's afraid of him!"

"*You're* the one we're humoring, listening to all this! *I* saw Rowena — does that make me crazy, too?"

Their eyes met and held. Kate saw the regret behind the glasses . . . the pity . . . and she started for the door.

"Kate, come one, they're just theories!"

"I don't like your theories, Denzil. I think they're stupid and insensitive."

"Kate!"

She put her hands over her ears and ran, his words echoing over and over in her mind. She didn't want to think about it anymore — *couldn't* think about it anymore — she'd go crazy with fear and doubts and questions —

Rowena could be anywhere. As Kate slowed to a walk, her stomach churned in sudden dread. And would it come without warning, some terrible surprise, would it be quick — *being aware of the horror but not believing, not ever believing it could happen to me* —

She locked her door and huddled there in her cabin, in the dark, afraid to move, to think, afraid to even leave again. *Why didn't I ask Tawney if I could stay with her tonight? Kate, you're so stupid!* Maybe she could just get a ride to the village, catch the train back — *but it's a joke, I'm playing right into their hands, getting scared, running away, giving them the satisfaction.* But what about Merriam? Had Merriam run away, too, had Merriam known what was happening when the fire started, *when she couldn't get out* —

"Kate? Kate, are you in there?"

"Tawney!" Flinging open the door, Kate hugged her friend tightly, trying not to cry as Tawney patted her gently on the back.

"Oh, Kate, I don't think you should stay here. Let's go back to my cabin, okay?"

"Yes," Kate said gratefully. "Yes. I'm so glad you thought of it."

She grabbed some things and within minutes

they set off. Tawney was rambling on about a new poem she'd written when Kate suddenly grabbed her arm.

"Tawney, do you hear something?"

The other girl stopped beside her and tilted her head, listening. "I don't think so. Why? Do you?"

"I . . . I'm not sure. . . ." Keeping hold of Tawney's arm, Kate started walking again, then froze almost immediately. "There," she whispered. "Just now."

Tawney's eyes grew large, and she looked around in alarm. "What is it?" she mouthed.

Kate took another hesitant step . . . stopped . . . listened. Her grip tightened on Tawney, and she gave her a shove.

"Someone's following us!" she hissed. "Run!"

Stumbling over each other, they didn't look back until they were safely inside Tawney's cabin. Kate leaned her head against the wall and closed her eyes, so weak she could hardly stand.

As a knock came suddenly at the door, they both jumped, and Kate forced herself to sound calm.

"Who is it?"

"Me," said Denzil. "Let me in."

Kate yanked open the door. "Denzil, *where* have you been?"

Denzil looked from Kate to Tawney and back again. "What do you mean? What's going on?"

"Someone was following us — back there in the woods." Kate tried to peer around him to search the dark clearing beyond. "You must have seen someone — they sounded so close — "

For a moment Denzil looked mystified. "I did see someone on the road. Just now, on my way from the kitchen." And as Tawney and Kate stared at him, he shook his head slowly. "It was really too dark," he said uncomfortably, "but . . . I think . . ." His voice trailed off, but Kate filled in the pieces.

"It was Gideon," she murmured. "Wasn't it?"

And even though she felt ready to drop, she knew she wouldn't be able to sleep tonight.

The morning dawned gloomy. Standing with her forehead against the windowpane, Kate saw the sun's futile struggle for survival as it drowned helplessly in swirls of gray clouds.

"That horror hunt thing's tonight," Tawney said, slipping into her clothes. "Maybe it'll rain and they'll call it off. Are you going?"

Kate shrugged apathetically. "I don't know. Do we have to?"

"Denzil says they're fun. But then" — she frowned — "Denzil has a pretty strange sense of humor."

Kate had to smile. "Denzil's strange — period."

"When I first knew him, I thought he was really funny 'cause he was always complaining about Gideon Drewe and his class and how much he hated it, only he kept going. Even after Gideon told him how untalented he was. You know what I think?"

"What do you think?"

"I think Denzil wants to get back at Gideon. I think Denzil wants to prove to Gideon how smart he is — no, smart's maybe not the best word. Clever . . . or . . . or sly. He told me once that he'd love to write a mystery where he'd have everybody completely fooled and the ending would be totally unexpected."

Buttoning her shirt, Kate paused, raising an eyebrow. "Denzil said that?"

"Yes, lots of times. And I bet he does it someday. He's just that stubborn. Oh, well" — Tawney stretched and yawned — "I'd better get to work. What are you doing today?"

"I don't know." Kate finished dressing and took another look at the dreary sky. "I have class this afternoon, and I'd like to drop in on Miss Bunceton again if I can get a ride."

"Someone's probably going," Tawney assured her. "I'll ask around."

"Thanks." Kate reached out and hugged her. "And thanks for letting me stay."

"That's okay," Tawney insisted. "Just plan on staying with me for the rest of the conference."

Kate felt a little better as they walked to the dining hall. Denzil didn't seem to be anywhere around, and after one look at the busy kitchen crew, Kate didn't think anyone would be going into the village. Deciding to check in the lodge, she told Tawney good-bye and was surprised to see Gideon out front getting into the van. She stared at his bent head, his hand on the door. *It was really too dark to see. . . .* Of course it could have been anyone that Denzil had spotted on the road last night, anyone at all, and even if it *had* been Gideon, that certainly didn't prove he'd been following her. He owned the camp, after all . . . he could go anywhere he pleased . . . *nothing suspicious about that. . . .*

"Good morning."

Kate started, so preoccupied with her own thoughts that she hadn't realized she'd been seen. Gideon's smile was tired. There was a gauntness to his face and his eyes looked hollow.

"Morning." She took a step closer, returning his smile with a thin one of her own. "Where are you off to so early?"

"To get Pearce. He called me last night — I think he's feeling rather desperate."

About you, Kate wanted to say, but didn't. "They're not going to let him come home so soon, are they?"

"I told you they'd be begging me to take him off their hands." He gave a dry laugh. "Anyway, he can rest as well here as there, and his mood will be very much improved, I've no doubt."

"Is there room for me to come with you?" Kate asked. "I'd like to make sure Miss Bunceton's doing okay."

"Of course. I'd be glad for the company." He opened the door and then hesitated, finally turning to face her. "Kate . . . I'm sorry for yesterday. I was feeling . . . well . . . overwhelmed. I shouldn't have burdened you the way I did. It's just been . . ." He seemed at a loss for words, and Kate touched his arm.

"It's all right," she said. "You don't have to be sorry about anything." She gazed deep into his eyes and felt herself drawn into their violet depths — deeper — deeper — and *what secrets are there, Gideon? What secrets do you know that I don't, or are you a victim just like me?*

"Kate? Are you all right?"

"Yes." He was holding her arms, holding her up, and she hadn't even realized how dizzy she was all of a sudden.

"Maybe you should go back inside. Did you eat breakfast?"

"I'm fine." He was studying her so intently that she managed a smile and pulled free. "I promise I won't faint on you."

"Well . . ." He smiled back. "I promise I'll look after you if you do."

They didn't say much on the ride to the clinic. Pearce was in his usual surly humor when they got there, and though Kate tried to pretend his indifference didn't matter, deep down it still hurt and confused her. She didn't want to admit to herself that she liked him as much as she did, but ever since the night of his injury, her feelings for him had changed. Pearce and Gideon were so different, so opposite in every way — and now, being with both of them at the same time was uncomfortable. She felt transparent somehow, and wondered if her attraction for each was picked up by the other. She was glad to escape to Miss Bunceton's room where they laughed and joked awhile — but when Gideon came for her, a strange trepidation fluttered in the pit of her stomach. She just couldn't seem to shake the feeling that something bad was going to happen.

Gideon pulled the van in front while Kate and a nurse helped Pearce to the curb. It was an easy matter to get Pearce situated comfortably on blankets in the back, and as the nurse left, Kate tucked an extra quilt around him while he scowled and tried to shove it off. Determined, Kate tucked it around again, and Gideon stood by impatiently, waiting to close the door.

"Kate, you dropped this." Gideon stooped and picked up a piece of paper that had fallen open on the floor next to Pearce.

Kate turned in surprise. "What? I don't think that's — " And as her hand went automatically to her shirt pocket, she saw Gideon's expression freeze, zeroed in on the paper, even as her own face went pale.

"Where'd this come from?" he murmured, and Pearce was staring, too, at the slow strange emotion crawling over Gideon's face. "Where did you get this, Kate — answer me!" His arm flew out and caught her, and she gave a cry of pain and surprise.

"Gideon, let go!"

"Why didn't you *tell* me about this?"

"I was *going* to — I *was*! Only you had so much on your mind and I didn't want to — "

Pearce was staring as if Gideon had lost his mind. "Gideon, let her go! Can't you see you're hurting her?"

"Read this." Gideon's voice was calm now, cold, chilling calm, as he thrust the paper beneath Pearce's nose. "Read it," he said. "*Read* it!"

Pearce scanned the note, his eyes, his hands faltering. He shook his head, his voice scarcely a whisper. "No . . ."

"She *is* alive, isn't she?" Gideon said flatly. And then suddenly his hands were on Pearce's shoulders, lifting him from the floor, and Kate was screaming but he didn't seem to hear, just lifting Pearce and pinning him back against the wall while Pearce moaned in pain. "*Isn't* she?! *She's alive, isn't she?*"

"*Yes!*" Pearce shouted. And as Gideon's hold on him loosened, he fell back upon the blanket, his face sweaty and ghostly pale, his eyes dark and haunted and . . . scared. "Yes, Gideon, yes, that's what you want to hear, isn't it? That's what you want me to say, isn't it? Well, now you know. Now you know at last." His eyes, black and wide and frighteningly empty, flashed to Gideon's face. "Yes," he whispered. "Yes. Rowena is alive."

Silence fell, sick and frightening. From some remote corner of her mind, Kate stared out at the strange tableau — Pearce lying back on the floor as if all the life were drained from him . . . Gideon now in the driver's seat, head bent upon the steering wheel, shoulders slumped . . . *and me . . . sitting here in the middle of all this madness, waiting for someone to kill me . . . waiting to die. . . .*

She was surprised at how calm she felt. So calm that it seemed hours had dragged by, yet the clock on the dash told her that they had sat there only minutes. . . .

"Where is she?" Gideon said at last.

Pearce shrugged and turned his head away.

"I need to know where she is. She's threatened Kate."

"I . . . I know." Pearce stared at the floor, and Gideon whirled in his seat, his voice seething.

"You have a lot of explaining to do, Pearce. But right now I'm concerned about Kate and her safety. I need to know how bad this all is — if Rowena's where we least expect it — "

"You won't find her in any crowd," Pearce said softly. "She . . . doesn't have a face."

"Oh, my God." Gideon made a choking sound in his throat and bent his head, taking deep breaths. "Tell me where she is."

"It won't do you any good," Pearce said hollowly. "She'll never want you to be happy . . . or love anyone . . . or have a good life . . . because hers is ruined — "

"Tell me," Gideon said again. His hands grabbed Pearce's shoulders, shook them. "Where *is* she?"

"She'll never let you go," said Pearce. "Or me. We'll never *really* be free of her, Gideon, you know that — "

"I know I'm afraid for Kate!" Gideon's voice rose. "And I don't want her hurt, no matter *what* I have to do. I know I haven't cared about *anyone* in a long time the way I care for Kate — "

"Then why don't you tell her the truth!" Pearce burst out. "About Rowena and the way things were! That Rowena was crazy — that you and William were *hiding* her! That the reason no one got her out is because no one even knew she was there! Go on! Tell Kate about Rowena! Why you two looked so much alike — because you were *twins*! *Tell her!* How you locked Rowena up because she was *insane*!"

As Kate looked on in silent horror, Gideon's hands slowly fell from Pearce's shoulders, his face rigid and pale as their eyes locked and held. For a long time there was no sound at all in the van . . . and then, at last, Pearce dropped his head and spoke.

"I know you care about Kate, Gideon. I care about her, too." Immediately his eyes shifted away, away from Kate and Gideon and their shocked stares. "Since the very first time I saw her, I . . ." He took a shaky breath. "I'm sorry, Gideon. It's not her fault she's caught up in this."

Gideon stared at him.

"Rowena *did* kill William, didn't she?"

"I think so."

"Have you found him?"

For another long moment there was silence. "Parts of him," Pearce said at last.

"My God . . . we have to go to the police."

"You can't do that. You can't tell anyone. We'll have to handle it ourselves."

"Pearce" — Gideon leaned forward again, his expression pleading — "where is she? You've got to tell me. Where . . . is . . . Rowena?"

Something crept across Pearce's face . . . something like a shadow . . . a sad, sad smile. "Don't you know, Gideon?" he whispered. "Don't you?"

Kate heard the motor rev up, felt the van tear out of the driveway.

She stared at Pearce, but he wouldn't look at her the rest of the way.

Chapter 19

When the van finally reached camp, Gideon dropped off Kate at the dining hall with a specific set of instructions.

"I want you to stay with your friends, understand? Don't go *anywhere* alone, not anywhere."

Kate looked at him beseechingly, keeping her voice low. "Can't I stay with you?"

"No. The *worst* thing you could do right now is be with me, *or* Pearce. Stay with your friends."

He started to pull away, but once more she stopped him. "Do you . . . think you know where she is?"

He leaned out the window and gazed off into the thick, tangled woods. "I'll just have to wait until she's ready to show herself," he murmured and was gone.

Kate couldn't find Denzil or Tawney anywhere. After a thorough search of the dining hall and their cabins, she found another employee who thought they might have gone into the village on errands. With Gideon's warning ringing in her ears, she hung around the kitchen for a while, then sat on the lodge porch pretending to read a magazine and nearly jumping out of her skin every time the door opened and closed. She couldn't keep her eyes off the trees, the cabin windows, the shadows hovering beside the road. She almost cried with relief when she saw Denzil and Tawney drive in with several other kids, then jump out, as the car sped away again.

"Hi, Kate!" Tawney waved. "Come in and have some ice cream!"

"Hey, kiddo, we looked for you." Denzil grinned. "We got some time off and saw a movie — where were you, anyway?"

Kate stared at him and said nothing as Tawney went inside.

"Actually, you didn't miss much. It was your standard run-of-the-mill horror story, right? Boy meets girl . . . boy butchers girl . . . boy — " He broke off as Kate flung her arms around him, squeezing his breath away. "Hey — what's wrong?"

"Oh, Denzil" — her voice was muffled against his shirt, but he could still hear the fear — "Rowena's alive. She killed William."

"Whoa!" He squirmed out of her grasp, his eyes as big as his glasses. "What did you — ?"

"And now she's after me. Pearce didn't want me to tell, but — "

"Wait. Back up. Start over. Nice and easy." He listened while Kate related the whole thing. Tawney poked her head out the door, but he waved her back inside. "Let's keep this quiet," he warned Kate.

"Tawney'll see psychos in every shadow."

"Oh, Denzil, what should I do?" Kate looked near tears, and Denzil put an arm around her, sitting her down on the steps. "Gideon dropped me off and told me to stay with you — that it'd be too dangerous right now to be with him or Pearce."

"Considerate guy." Denzil grunted. "Well, he's right about one thing — being with people is probably best. She's not likely to try anything with an audience, I would think."

"The horror hunt's tonight," Kate reminded him. "I don't want to stay in camp by myself, but I don't want to be wandering around out there, either."

Denzil thought a minute. "It'd probably be safer if you went. We'll be working in teams, so you'll be with us."

"Denzil, I'm so scared — I haven't done anything — why is this happening to *me*? I mean, I just came here to learn something about writing and to have some fun, that's all — Denzil?"

Denzil was looking at her as if he hadn't heard a word she'd said. Impatiently Kate shook his arm.

"Did you hear me? *You're* scaring me. What's wrong?"

He opened his mouth as if to answer, then seemed to change his mind. Behind the round glasses, his eyes squinted, troubled.

"Something," he mumbled. "Something's not quite right."

Kate stared at him, a humorless laugh bursting out. "Well, thank you, Sherlock Holmes — what an absolutely *brilliant* deduction!"

Denzil got up and walked a few steps . . . tapped his fist absently against one upturned palm . . . walked back again. "For one thing . . . where did Pearce take Rowena after she was burned?"

"I don't know."

"If she was burned so badly that she lost her face, people around here would know about it."

"Then he had to have taken her somewhere else. Another town. Maybe another state."

"But why?"

Kate looked blank. "Because . . . she never wanted anyone to know? Or maybe Pearce couldn't stand having other people see how hideous she looked? Anyway, if they'd been hiding her, he couldn't have risked anyone finding out about her."

Denzil nodded slowly, still walking, still thinking. "So where does Pearce hide her now?"

"Well . . . maybe in his house . . . or the main house . . . there must be tons of places around here — the woods, the cabins, all these buildings around everywhere — "

"Yeah." He sighed, taking off his hat, running one hand through his hair. "It's just . . . I don't know. . . ."

"Tragic," Kate finished. "I hope Gideon's going to the police right now."

"What a scandal," Denzil mused. "*If* they find her. Hell, if the police come in, she may *never* come out of hiding."

"So what happens in the meantime?"

"I'm sticking to you like needles on a cactus,"

Denzil said. "She'll either give up, or you'll lure her out of hiding."

"Great. You mean use me as bait."

"I can't get you away tonight — at least not till later. A bunch of the workers went dancing and took all the cars. But first thing in the morning, I'm getting you on that train."

Kate thought a moment. "I can't run away, Denzil."

"Why not?"

"Because she might follow me. Or find me. Then I'd always have to be afraid."

"Somehow I can't picture a black corpse traveling incognito." Denzil attempted a smile. "And anyway, I thought you liked to be scared."

"Not when it's real," Kate said seriously. "Not when I can't just close the book or leave the movie or turn off the TV. And if I run away now, I'd always have to *wonder*. Wonder if she followed me . . . or if she's on the phone when I pick it up . . . or if she's waiting around the very next corner."

"Kate," Denzil said, "that's pretty unlikely."

"Not for Merriam it wasn't." She stared at him and saw the slight pallor of his cheeks though his head was turned. "You know now, don't you? That it wasn't suicide? And if Rowena found Merriam . . . then she could find me."

The door burst open, and they both jumped. Tawney beamed and handed each of them an ice cream cone.

"I lost a contact," she warned them. "So if you

bite down on something hard, it's not a pecan."

"Thanks." Denzil eyed the cone suspiciously, then glanced at his watch. "Hey, the horror hunt's starting — we'd better hurry." As Tawney walked ahead, he reached for Kate's hand, brought it to his lips, and kissed it. "You're something," he said seriously. "I'm not gonna let anything happen to you."

Kate couldn't speak. She squeezed his hand, and they went into the lodge, where an instructor was going over the game rules.

"No one is to go outside the camp boundaries or off the main trails. Everything on the list can be found somewhere on the grounds. And each of you gets a flashlight, if you don't already have one. Any more questions?"

"What about a time limit?" someone spoke up.

"Two hours. Everyone should meet back here then. If you don't, we'll assume you're lost and gone forever."

There was a ripple of laughter around the room, and Tawney looked at Kate.

"That's not funny. I wouldn't want to be lost out there."

"Me, neither."

"Why, there could be anything out there." Tawney frowned. "Wild animals . . . people who've escaped from mental institutions — "

"Ssh!" Denzil hissed. "I'm trying to listen!"

" — into groups," the instructor went on. "Here are the lists and extra maps. The team with the most points wins."

"That'll be us," Denzil said confidently. "We can't lose."

"Who made up the list?" someone called out.

The instructor quickly consulted another man beside him. "We think Gideon Drewe — we're not sure."

"Where *is* Gideon Drewe, anyway?"

"We're not sure about that, either." The instructor laughed. "He was supposed to be here, but he hasn't shown up."

"Then let's get going." Denzil jumped up and led the way over to the lists and flashlights.

"I want one," said Tawney. "What's it say?"

Kate peeked over Denzil's shoulder, quickly scanning the list. "Something dead. Something a hangman uses. A murder weapon. Something you can't escape — "

"Something you can't escape. . . ." Tawney's face lit up. "I know! Spiderwebs!"

"Quit giving away all our ideas." Denzil jerked the list away before Kate could finish reading. "Hurry up, everyone else has started." As he and Tawney headed for the door, Kate picked up a list of her own and read it as she walked.

"There are so many weird things on here," she mumbled.

"Yeah, and different points for each one." Denzil followed Tawney outside. "Let's do the ones with the most points first."

"Come on!" Tawney stamped her feet excitedly. "This is going to be so — Kate, are you all right?"

But Kate didn't hear her, and she didn't see Denzil's puzzled stare as her eyes went down the list, down to the item at the bottom of the page, the item typed in big bold letters, the item worth the most points of all —

"Teacher's pet," she whispered, and Denzil was beside her in an instant, trying to take the paper, trying to pry it out of her hands. "Teacher's pet!" Kate said again, only this time it was a cry coming up from the back of her throat.

"Kate," Denzil said sternly, and at last he tore the paper free. "Kate, stop it — *stop*!"

They stood there facing each other, and Tawney wedged in between them, anxiously turned toward Kate.

"I saw that, Kate, but I don't think it means what you're thinking — not a *person* — I think they mean *Pet*. You know, the cat — 'cause, really, he's William's cat, and all the things on the list are *trick* things; they sort of don't mean what they seem. . . ." She looked pleadingly at Kate and shook her gently by the shoulders. "Aren't I right, Kate? It's just a *fun* thing, and anyway" — she glanced around and lowered her voice — "I saw Gideon yesterday in the lodge, and we were talking about puns and things, and Pet was curled up in his lap — and I said, oh-ho, look at the teacher's pet — so I think he maybe used my idea." She stepped back, pleased, but when Kate didn't respond, her face grew troubled again. "I'm pretty sure this is fun, Kate. Really . . ."

"Nice going, Tawney." Denzil glared at her.

"Come on," Kate said shakily. "We're wasting time."

After a hurried discussion, they decided on a bone for the "something dead." There'd been chicken for dinner so there were plenty of scraps in the garbage behind the dining hall. Tawney scooped up a clump of spiderwebs from underneath one of the cabin porches, and Denzil raided the toolshed and got a rusty metal file for their murder weapon. Everyplace they went, they kept a lookout for Pet, but the cat didn't seem to be anywhere around.

"She's probably at Gideon's house," Tawney said at last. "Maybe we should look there."

Huddled over their flashlights, Kate and Denzil reviewed their lists again and acted like they didn't hear.

"So, what next?" Denzil prompted, glancing off into the trees. "Something that crawls? A pentagram? Remember, we need *points*."

For all his show of joviality, Kate sensed it was forced. He hadn't stopped watching her since they'd left the lodge, and more than once as she'd looked nervously off into the shadows, she'd caught him doing the same thing.

"The cat," Tawney said again. "Don't you think we should be looking for Pet?"

"We'll find her," Denzil said evasively. "Don't worry about it. Just come on." He grabbed Kate's elbow and frowned. "Do you wanna go back to my cabin and rest awhile? You don't look too good — "

"No. I'm fine." She stared at him, with a tight smile. Denzil had a funny look on his face.

"Maybe you'd better sit down — "

"What's next?" Kate asked quickly. *Keep moving. Don't think.*

Denzil took a step closer. "Look, I really mean it, maybe you should — "

"Denzil, I am all *right*," Kate said sharply. "Just get on with the hunt and stop nagging me."

Denzil flushed and dropped back. Both he and Tawney stared at her, and Kate looked guiltily away.

"Hey, that's cool." Denzil held up his hands. "Whatever you say, Kate."

Kate swallowed over the lump in her throat. "Denzil, I'm sorry — " she began, but he and Tawney had already moved down the path ahead of her.

Kate wasn't sure what they were looking for now, nor did she care. She followed them, head down, feet dragging, a terrible fear growing inside her. . . .

"Something an executioner would carry." Tawney's voice drifted back. "An axe?"

Even from a distance, Kate could hear Denzil's tension. "Nah, that's too easy. Everyone'll think of — " He stopped so abruptly on the path that Kate ran into him. But as she looked up, his gaze was directed somewhere over her head. "Do you smell something?" he asked sharply. "Smoke?"

Tawney sniffed the air. "No. Just cold."

"Smoke," Denzil said again. He was already heading down the path, his head swiveling from side to side. "It's smoke. I'm sure it's smoke — "

"It's the fireplace in the lodge, probably," Tawney said. "I don't think anyone's burning leaves out here tonight, do you?"

But Denzil was going faster now, his face tilted to the sky. "It's not the fireplace, it's something else."

As her friends moved away, Kate made an effort to shake off her sluggishness and follow. The crisp night air sliced into her lungs, yet suddenly the back of her throat began to burn.

Denzil froze on the path, his glance alarmed as he shouted back over his shoulder. "It *is* fire! It's one of the cabins!"

The next thing Kate knew, they were all running, racing down the path, as an orangish glow suddenly shone through the trees ahead. She heard Tawney scream, and her heart leaped into her throat.

"Oh, Kate!" Tawney screamed again. "It's *your* cabin!"

And Kate saw the flames then, licking from the doorway, the throbbing, flickering pulse of fire as it crept over and through the little house.

"No!" she screamed.

In unthinking panic, she bolted for the door and went down as someone tackled her from behind.

"Are you *crazy*?" Denzil shouted. "What're you *doing*?"

She kicked at him. "Let me go!"

"You can't go in there, it's too late!"

As Kate stared helplessly at the growing inferno, Tawney sank down beside her and began to cry.

"What'd you do, Kate?" Denzil yelled, practically beside himself. "Leave your heater on?"

"I didn't do *anything!" Rowena did. Rowena set this on purpose because Gideon and Pearce belong to her. . . .*

"I'm calling the fire department!" Denzil whirled to go, then turned back to the girls huddled there on the ground. "Tawney," he ordered, "call Gideon. Use the phone in the lodge — the number's in the office."

Tawney jumped up, scared and confused. "What . . . what should I tell him?"

Taking off, Denzil spun back. "Tell him there's an emergency! Tell him to get his butt down here!"

"Come on!" Kate jumped up and ran with Tawney to the lodge. Already people had begun to smell the smoke, temporarily abandoning the hunt to seek out the source of the fire. As Tawney dialed the number and gripped the phone to her ear, Kate paced back and forth, mentally counting the number of rings. After several moments, Tawney held the receiver out to her.

"Oh, Kate," she cried, "no one's answering! What'll I do?"

"But he's home!" Kate grabbed the phone away. "They're *both* home! Someone should answer — "

Three rings. Seven. Five more. Kate slammed down the receiver, pulling Tawney toward the door.

"Come on," she cried, "you have to come with me, okay?"

"Where are we going?"

"To Gideon's house. Something's wrong — "

"But shouldn't we wait for Denzil?"

"No, no, there's no time. Just hurry!"

She prayed she'd remember the way. She prayed for a bad phone line and that Pearce and Gideon just hadn't heard the ringing, she prayed that she'd have enough courage to go into that house, not knowing what she might find —

The gate was open when they got there. The house loomed up dark and silent, and Tawney pressed close to Kate.

"That's where Gideon lives?"

"Yes. But there should be lights, and the gate's not usually open. I've got to go in, Tawney. I'm afraid — "

"What's that?" Tawney's voice dropped, and she glanced uneasily over her shoulder. "Did you hear something?"

Kate was instantly alert. She swept her flashlight through the darkness and reached for Tawney's hand. "I don't hear anything. What did it sound like?"

"Something moving. I don't know . . . something."

Please, God, just let it be the wind. "I don't hear it."

"Let's go," Tawney whispered. "I don't like this."

"You can wait here for me. If I'm not out in five minutes — "

"No, I'll come with you." Tawney tried to sound brave. "Only, let's hurry, okay?"

Kate nodded and they went slowly toward the house . . . up the steps . . . across the porch to the door. Raising her hand, Kate gave a timid knock. A blast of cold whirled a shower of leaves around their feet, and Tawney stifled a scream. Kate knocked again. The door rattled in its frame, but nobody answered.

"I think we should leave now," Tawney said. "I don't think anybody's home."

Kate backed off the porch and hesitated, listening for some sound within. If Rowena *did* come back, surely they would have overpowered her, even with Pearce's injuries — surely — *unless she surprised them, unless she caught them off guard and it's too late, neither of them can help me now —*

"Tawney?" Kate's voice trembled, and she turned around.

Tawney wasn't there.

"*Tawney!*" Kate screamed. "Tawney, where *are* you?"

And she heard the front door opening . . . squeaking back on its hinges . . . and the soft moan . . . like someone in pain. . . .

"Pearce?" Kate called, alarmed. "Pearce, is that you? Are you all right? Where's — ?"

"Kate," the voice whispered, floating from the yawning black hole of a doorway. "You shouldn't have come here. . . ."

"Gideon?"

Fearfully Kate moved toward his voice . . . felt her feet cross the threshold . . . saw a shadowy figure hovering near the stairs at the end of the hall.

"Gideon? Is that you? There's been a fire and — "

Her voice faded as she stared at him. In the sickly

glow of her flashlight, his face seemed unnaturally pale, his body propped against the wall as if standing were too great an effort.

In his hands he held a long, black piece of cloth.

A veil.

Numbness went through her. Her eyes locked on his blurred face . . . his eyes, deep holes without color. . . .

"Gideon . . ."

"You can't have either one of us, you see." His voice was a hollow whisper. The veil moved between his fingers as he came slowly toward her. "Not me . . . not Pearce . . . Rowena would never allow that. If Rowena can't love, then no one can."

Kate felt herself stumbling, slow-motion panic pulling her back, her body blocked by the wall. *My God . . . my God . . . Gideon. . . .*

"It's not your fault that you're so beautiful," he whispered, and still he moved closer, the long black material like a rope in his hands, twisting, turning . . . "that you're so easy to fall in love with. . . ."

"No . . ." Kate flattened herself against the wall . . . watched him come closer. "Gideon . . . no. . . ."

Terror exploded behind her eyes. Through a haze, she saw the walls sway around her . . . the ceiling tilt crazily above her head. A swirl of images flooded her mind — *Teacher's pet . . . Gideon twisting the axe in the tree . . . slashed clothes . . . "Rowena would be jealous of that" . . . the eyes at her window . . . blood . . . blood . . . blood everywhere . . . and "inseparable" Pearce had said . . . "twins"*

. . . *"closer than anyone could guess"* . . . *"he still hasn't gotten over it . . . I don't think he ever will".* . . .

"What's the matter with you?!" Kate screamed. "Why are you looking at me like that!"

"Don't you understand," Gideon murmured, and still he came, twisting the black softness in his hands, like smoke, like killing smoke. . . . "Don't you see? If she can't have her own life, then you can't have yours. And I . . . can't have mine."

"Pearce!" Kate pleaded. "Pearce, help me!"

Gideon stopped. He swayed a little, one hand reaching for the wall. "Pearce can't help you," he said sadly. "Pearce is dead."

"Oh, God — " Kate's mind raced, her body inching sideways along the wall. She saw the huge vase on the table, and Gideon's bewildered face as she grabbed the vase and held it above her head. She saw his eyes widen and the shape of his mouth, the silent "no" as she flung the vase at his skull. His body teetered only a second, then collapsed onto the floor.

Kate stood for a moment, looking down at him, fighting back a sudden wave of nausea. *Oh, Gideon . . . Gideon . . . why. . . ?* It was so hot in here, so hot and cold at the same time, and that smell, that funny smell, like dead, dried flowers and something else . . . something bad and terrible . . . creeping through the hall. . . .

Creeping down the stairs.

Slowly . . . in a numbness of sickening horror . . . Kate raised her eyes. . . .

And saw Rowena looking down at her.

"It can't be," Kate mumbled, but no sound came out, no sound, no screaming, not even a breath of air. "No, it's impossible." And Rowena was close now, so very close, the strange odor all around her now, that unbearable sickness, closing off her throat, her lungs. . . . "Gideon, wake up," but the plea was in her mind, only in her head. "Gideon, I'm so sorry — "

And she couldn't look away, she couldn't turn her face from that black veil and the faceless thing behind it, the horrible stench filling her nostrils as Rowena reached into the pocket of her long black skirt . . . the hideous thing lying in her black-gloved palm . . . its rotting fingers outstretched in silent agony. . . .

William Drewe's hand.

"No!" Kate shrieked. "*NO!*" And with one swipe, she knocked it to the floor, the splayed, decaying fingers clawing toward her, the hand reaching out for her, and Kate could see it was *moving*, pulling itself across the floor, trying to touch her, and *my God, it's on the back of my neck now, behind me, how could it be behind me? Oh, God, the back of my head* —

In a dizzying panic, Kate realized that there *was* a hand on her head, around her neck, pressing itself over her nose and windpipe, and the great waves of suffocation plummeting her down a long, dark tunnel. . . .

She saw Rowena's huge, blank eyes. . . .

And then they drew her in, and all was darkness.

Chapter 20

Help me, someone. Denzil? Gideon? Anyone . . . please. . . .

Kate was aware of her own consciousness drifting slowly around her, just beyond reach. From far away someone called her name . . . an empty, unearthly sound . . . as if it came from some soulless being. . . .

Yes. I'm here, but something's wrong. Help me . . . please. . . .

The sound of her voice roused her, the words fading in her mind. She realized she hadn't actually spoken at all, yet she was awake. She realized she was conscious again, yet she couldn't see a thing.

Groggily Kate tried to move and felt pains in her arms and legs. Her head weighed a ton, and her muscles were twisted at unnatural angles. She moved her fingers and something dug into her wrists. Beneath the blindfold she was suddenly aware of lying spread-eagled upon a bed, her hands and feet securely bound to the bedposts. In a split second every nightmare came true, and she gave a cry as she tried to wrench free.

"I'm glad you're awake," said a voice, and it was very near her, so calm in the silence of the room. "I wouldn't want you to miss a single thing."

She recognized the hoarse, strained whisper. An icy dread pumped through her, and she lay still, trying to keep her face expressionless.

"We don't have to hurry," Rowena went on. "We have lots of time. There's no one to bother us."

Tears pressed behind Kate's eyelids, and she fought them back.

"Please let me go. I haven't done anything to you."

From somewhere deep in Rowena's throat came a laugh. "Kate, Kate, teacher's pet, as frightened as can be . . . no matter how you run and hide . . . you can't escape from me."

"Please, Rowena . . . *please* — "

"And you're wrong about not having done anything."

Slow footsteps approached the bed . . . stopped a distance away.

"You're so beautiful." The voice sounded wistful and sad. "Like I used to be. With all the hope . . . the future . . . that I used to have. . . ." Beneath the hoarseness, tears crept in. "Did you know that Pearce loved me once? We were going to be married . . . but who could live with a face like mine now?"

"He still loves you," Kate whispered, "he never stopped loving you — "

"To look into my face," Rowena murmured, "is to see a glimpse of hell." The voice tightened. "So he fell in love with you."

"No . . . no, he didn't — "

"You *had* Gideon . . . but then you wanted Pearce, too — "

"No!"

"Do you think I could let you have them? *Either* of them? Who would love *me*? Who would take care of *me*?"

Kate's mind raced desperately. She couldn't hear Rowena anymore, couldn't tell where she was, and Kate fought to keep from screaming out loud.

"Rowena," Kate lifted her head, searching for the sound of footsteps . . . breathing. . . . "I'm leaving again in a few days — *tomorrow*, if you like — you'll have both of them all to yourself — "

Oh, God, you killed Pearce . . . Pearce is dead —

"Pearce took care of me, but William found out." Rowena was rambling on again, pacing beside the bed. "I *had* to get rid of him. He found out, and he was going to send me away — "

"Rowena, *listen* to me, I'll leave tonight if you like — I'll never tell anybody I saw you — no one will ever know — "

"Yes," she said. "Yes. You're leaving, Kate. Tonight."

The footsteps stopped. In the terrible silence, Kate lay motionless. The voice spoke again, leaving a trail of breath along one of Kate's outstretched arms.

"Kate . . . Kate . . . don't you cry. . . ." The whisper hesitated . . . laughed . . . "Pretty Kate . . . it's time to die. . . ."

The voice faded.

A hand touched Kate's forehead, and she whimpered in terror.

"Please . . . please don't hurt me."

"But I have to hurt you. I have to. I want you to know how it feels . . . to lose everything."

Kate thrashed against the ropes, her scream echoing again and again through the silent house. Above her, Rowena laughed softly and caressed her cheek.

"Oh, God. . . ." Kate was crying now, the blindfold soaked with tears. She went limp upon the bed, and felt Rowena's fingers lightly stroking her face . . . her neck . . . running the length of her body.

"Will it help," Rowena asked softly, "if you watch yourself die? Like I watched the flames coming closer and closer? If you know what's coming, then perhaps you won't be so frightened."

Kate felt the blindfold tighten . . . grow loose . . . fall away.

It was so dark.

Blinking through tears and shadows, Kate saw that she was on the bed in Rowena's room, the heavy black bedcurtains between her and one dim lamp in the far corner. She saw the black walls . . . the black ceiling . . . she saw Rowena's arms reach out from the shadows to lift the bedcurtains aside. She saw the veil, rippling softly in and out with Rowena's breath.

"Gideon," Kate pleaded, her face covered with tears.

"Gideon can't save you now," Rowena said. "No one can."

One black glove lifted . . . teasingly . . . and the veil fluttered as the fingers worked to free it.

"No," Kate whispered, "please — "

With her other hand, Rowena grabbed Kate's face and held it. "Have a look," she hissed. "It's the last thing you'll see before you die."

And as Kate fought to look away, Rowena's veil slipped down to her shoulders . . . fluttered down to her feet . . . the twisted face leaning down, distorted in shadow —

"My God," Kate gasped. "*Pearce* — "

"And since you love to be scared, you'll enjoy this, Kate," Rowena said, Rowena's voice, Rowena's laugh, only it was Pearce — *Pearce* — who leaned down at her, dressed in Rowena's long, black clothes — "You'll enjoy this, because you won't die right away — "

"Pearce," Kate sobbed, "*please!* Let me go!"

The cold eyes narrowed. "Pearce can't help you! Pearce belongs to me!"

In one sudden movement, he crossed the room. Kate saw him grab something from the corner, heard the slosh of liquid, felt something wet and cold douse her body. She smelled the unmistakable fumes of gasoline, and in a macabre fury, Pearce twirled through the shadows, black clothes flying, the gasoline wetting down everything in his path.

"*Stop it!*" she was screaming, pleading, out of her mind with terror. "Don't do this! If you kill me, they'll take you away from here! Away from Pearce and Gideon!"

He froze in the middle of the room, eyes glaring,

gasping for breath. As he stared at her he slowly lowered the can, arms going limp at his sides. The can rolled across the floor.

"They can't separate us," Rowena's voice said numbly. "They can't. . . ."

"But they *will*! You'll never see them again! Never!"

For a long moment his head hung down . . . and then he smiled, half of his face showing in the light. "I didn't die that night, you know . . . in the fire? The fire that *Pearce* started. . . . He wanted to kill William, and I was going to help him . . . only William locked me in his room, and Pearce didn't know." The smile faltered, sad. "He didn't know, you see . . . it wasn't his fault. And I screamed . . . and screamed . . . but he didn't come. . . ."

"Don't . . ." Kate's lips moved, the room swimming through hopeless tears. "Don't . . ."

Pearce pulled a matchbook from his pocket.

"I didn't die that night. Pearce loves me. I would never leave him."

He struck the match sharply against the cover.

He held up the flame, its pulsing light reflected in his hollow eyes.

"He can't love you," Pearce said softly in Rowena's voice. "It's me he loves."

The flame descended, spreading behind his fingers as he held it out to the gasoline. . . .

Behind him shadows flickered wildly as the bedroom door creaked slowly on its hinges.

"Put it out, Pearce," the voice said. "Put it out now, or I swear I'll kill Rowena."

As Kate watched in stunned amazement, Gideon stepped into the room, moving Rowena in front of him — *the real Rowena* — dressed in black from head to toe, her bowed head draped with her long, black veil. Pearce froze and stared at them, the match burning dangerously close to his fingertips.

"Put it out," Gideon said again. His voice had never sounded so calm . . . so dangerous. "You won't be able to save her this time. This time she'll die, and you'll never see her again."

Confusion blanched Pearce's face. Like someone in a deep trance, he brought the match to his lips. . . .

Even from where she lay, Kate could see the flame beginning to lick at his fingers. She saw his hand jerk back . . . heard his exclamation of pain —

The match fell onto his shoe and fizzled out.

She saw him reach into his pocket. . . .

And pull out the matchbook once more.

"Don't," Gideon said. "I'm not bluffing. Rowena dies if you light that match."

With a sudden movement, he jerked Rowena back against him, her body trapped in the circle of his arms.

"You can't kill me," Pearce mumbled, sounding like Rowena, and suddenly he seemed unsure . . . frightened . . . "Pearce won't let you. . . ."

"Oh, but you're wrong. I'm doing it now. Just watch me." His hands tightened around Rowena's throat, and she slumped against him.

As a range of emotions struggled across his face,

Pearce looked in dismay from Kate to Rowena and back again.

"No," he mumbled, "no . . . I'm not . . . I'm . . ."

Gideon sprang at him, their bodies crashing to the floor. In the crazily throbbing shadows, they rolled back and forth through the gasoline. As Rowena fell against the door, someone began pounding and shouting from the other side, and through a haze of unbelieving terror, Kate saw Pearce jump up and throw Rowena aside as he jerked the door open and bolted through.

"Kate . . . are you all right?"

Gideon fumbled at the ropes around her wrists, and Kate could see stark fear etched upon every line of his face. As her bonds fell away, he grabbed her into his arms and held her as if he'd never let her go.

"Oh, Kate . . . oh, my dear Kate. . . ."

"Rowena," she could scarcely speak, "is . . . that Rowena? Is she really all right?"

"I'm all right," the girl said, and to Kate's astonishment Tawney stood up and pushed back the veil with a bewildered smile. "Oh, Kate, he could have *killed* you!"

"Kate! Kate!" As the door burst wide, Denzil raced in, braking to a stop as he saw Kate in Gideon's arms.

With a cavalier grin, Gideon stood aside and nodded. "Please . . . be my guest. You've certainly earned it."

Clutched tightly against Denzil's chest, Kate clung to him and cried while Gideon herded them all from the room. Out in the hallway, she looked into Denzil's eyes, trying to smile as he mopped at her face with his handkerchief.

"You're all cut up," she worried, reaching out gingerly to his forehead, to the blood trickling down his cheeks.

"It's nothing," Denzil brushed her off. "All in the line of duty."

"But look at you — you're really hurt."

"Yeah, he landed a few good punches." Denzil sighed, then fixed her with a lopsided grin. "But he's no match for me."

Over Denzil's shoulder Kate saw Pearce's body sprawled on the floor. Gideon examined it, then hoisted it over his shoulder and started down the stairs.

"Come on," Gideon insisted, "we've got to get out of here."

"Pearce," Kate mumbled, "is he — ?"

"Out cold," Denzil said, looking particularly proud of himself. And then at Kate's questioning look, he held out his broken hand. "Fastest fist in the west."

"Denzil, you are so weird."

"You're right."

"And" — she smiled, giving him a kiss — "so wonderful."

"Right again." He smiled back. "I thought you'd never notice."

Chapter 21

"I can never make it up to you," Gideon said. "Not after all the pain and disaster you've been through."

"Don't be silly." Kate smiled. "It wasn't your fault." She glanced over at Denzil and the van, hardly able to believe everything was over. "And after all, I caused *you* some pain, too."

"You did at that," Gideon nodded, rubbing the swollen place on his head. "What a pitcher you'd make — your aim is superb." He gave a wry grin. "And I should be very angry at you, anyway, suspecting me like you did, when all along . . ." His voice trailed away, the smile fading. "The doctors say it all began long ago, Pearce's obsession with Rowena. And then . . . when I had to be away . . . William must have made terrible threats, done horrible things to torment them. When Pearce set the fire to get rid of William and killed Rowena by mistake . . . well . . . there was no hope then. Killing William was inevitable . . . only a matter of time."

Kate shook her head. "So Pearce did confess. I'm so sorry, Gideon." She reached for his hand, her voice hesitant. "Then . . . will you ever be able to find William?"

Gideon made a harsh sound in his throat. "We'll probably never find all of him; Pearce — Rowena — scattered him all over camp, and can only recall a few of the graves. One by the lake . . . one near your cabin. One in the dumpster behind the lodge. . . ." He looked down, not seeing Kate's shudder.

"He's Pearce now. Sitting down there, talking to the doctors, he'll be Pearce for a while. He's been telling them all about Rowena and how he needs to come home to care for her because *I* have other interests and can't be depended upon when she needs someone. And he's telling them how jealous Rowena is of you . . . and how she'd kill you if she could. Just like she killed Merriam."

For a moment there was silence. Kate gently squeezed his fingers.

"She truly was brilliant, you know," Gideon said softly. "And truly mad. My parents simply couldn't face the truth of what she was . . . what she would always be. Yet they couldn't bring themselves to abandon her to some institution . . . and so they hid her away from the world." He nodded slightly, his face thoughtful. "So it really wasn't her fault, you see. It really wasn't. . . ."

Kate's fingertips brushed his cheek. "If you hadn't shown up when you did, I *would* be dead now. I know Pearce would have killed me. You saved my life."

"Your friend Tawney saved your life," Gideon

said modestly. "She ran back to find Denzil and suddenly realized you weren't behind her like she thought."

Kate chuckled. "It never occurred to me that she'd just leave."

"Denzil found me in the hall and got me moving again. He's the one who thought to go upstairs."

"You acted so strange when I saw you — it really scared me. That's why I thought — "

"That I was going to strangle you, wasn't that it? Well, I'm sure I was rather frightening," Gideon agreed. "Pearce had managed to drug my coffee with something he'd taken from the clinic. I don't know how long I was out — obviously long enough for him, as Rowena, to set fire to your cabin. Rowena was feeling desperate at that point — Pearce had admitted on the way home that he was attracted to you, and Rowena couldn't let that happen."

"But what about his foot? It must have been excruciating to walk on."

"Not really. As Rowena, he had no injuries. He felt no pain. As Pearce now, he's suffering for it."

"So that's when you knew? When you finally woke up?"

"I was still so disoriented when you got there — I was trying to make you understand what was happening, but I could hear myself going on, not making any sense to anyone but myself. No wonder I frightened you half to death. When I came to and realized Pearce had drugged me, and then found him missing, that's when I began to put two and two together. I remembered how he'd acted at the clinic. And while I was searching for him, that's when I discovered some of Rowena's things missing from her closet . . . and others that looked as if they'd been worn. I truly *did* think Pearce had died mentally at that point."

Kate shook her head, still stunned by the enormity of it all. "So who thought of using Tawney? You?"

"I wish I could take the credit for an original plot, but when I realized what danger you were in, my mind went absolutely blank. The truth is, it was all Denzil's idea." He smiled at that. "A masterful plan, really. We got Tawney into some of Rowena's clothes, and used the veil."

"She had *me* fooled." Kate couldn't help but laugh.

"And has some bruises for her trouble, I've no doubt." Gideon squeezed Kate's hand, his voice urgent. "It was Rowena, you know, Pearce as Rowena all along — your clothes, your cabin, all of it. He even admitted that Rowena set the trap for you by the cave . . . but caught the wrong person."

Kate looked away, a lump forming in her throat. "He was so sick that night . . . so . . . helpless. . . ."

"Yes . . . helpless . . ." Gideon looked down at her, a faint smile crossing his face. "And I was so worried about you . . . and in the process nearly succeeded in scaring you to death. That night at your window — "

"That *was* you!"

"Yes." He looked sheepish. "I wanted to make sure you were all right. I was trying to play the hero, guarding your cabin." He laughed at himself. "And I followed you, too — several times. Only you heard me, and that frightened you more. What a poor excuse for a bodyguard I'd make."

"I'm not complaining," Kate assured him with a smile.

Gideon let out a long, weary sigh. "Pearce wanted Rowena with him forever, you know. And now . . . I suppose . . . he has her. Kate . . . I . . ." He looked away, his voice softening. "Forever is such a big, frightening word. I'd be happy with just tomorrow. . . . to know you're there. . . ."

Kate studied his wonderful profile, her heart catching. "I'm not really so far away, you know. By plane. Or letter."

"Or telephone." He smiled. "Or even thought."

"As if you don't have enough on your mind already," Kate scolded. "And don't make promises you don't intend to keep."

"Oh, but I do intend to keep them — although I *will* have to get matters straightened out here first." His expression went serious, and Kate took his arm.

"You'll be fine," she said firmly. "You *will* be. And you have your writing — *your* books, not William's. And you'll have *lots* of others. I know it."

"Thank you. For that confidence. It means a lot." His eyes settled on hers, and he caressed her cheek . . . turned her face up . . . kissed her. "And so do you."

"Hey, Kate!" Denzil yelled. "The stagecoach is leaving! You coming?"

Kate grinned as Denzil waved his bandaged hand. Gideon grinned back at her and let out a groan.

"My competition again. He's very determined, you know — he won't give up easily."

"I've come to that conclusion." Kate laughed and threw her arms around him for one last hug. "Good-bye, Gideon. Thanks. For everything."

He watched her run to the van and shouted after her, "And keep writing! I'll be expecting to see your name on the bestseller list!"

"Jeez" — Denzil rolled his eyes — "doesn't that guy ever give up?"

"It's part of the courting ritual," Tawney said seriously. "I think I'll write a poem about it."

"No," Denzil groaned. "I know I'll be sorry I asked this, . . . but what's the title?"

" 'Passion's Wooing Takes Persistent Doing.' "

"I'm even sorrier than usual. Just drive."

Kate smiled out the window as they wound their way out of the woods and into the village. The air was fresh and pure, pine-fragrant and sun-warmed. As they pulled up to the depot, Miss Bunceton waved excitedly from the platform.

"Yoo-hoo! Kate, dear!"

"Oh, Miss Bunceton, you look like you feel better!"

"Gracious, yes. Now, you mustn't touch me . . . but *nothing* could have kept me in that bed another day!"

"I'm so sorry about your things," Kate said. "With the fire and all — "

"Good excuse to buy *new* things! I'm just glad *I* wasn't in the cabin when it went up — oh, look, there's our train!"

"Yes." Kate turned and looked at her friends, sudden tears in her eyes. "Good-bye, Tawney," she said, hugging the girl tightly. "Don't forget to write and send your poems. I'm sure going to miss you — oh, and I'll send your clothes back just as soon as I get home."

"They look better on you," Tawney insisted, her own eyes wet. "And I'll write, I promise."

"See you, kid." Denzil hugged her, eyes twinkling like an amused owl. "You've been one hell of a sidekick. Even if you do attract every man between here and the Rio Grande."

"Denzil — " Kate began, but suddenly felt her words smothered by his kiss.

"I'll find you," Denzil said, the corners of his mouth moving up in a grin. "I'll track you down."

"Come, Kate, let's board." Miss Bunceton bustled her up onto the train.

"There's no place big enough where you can hide!" Denzil yelled.

Kate laughed and waved as the train whistle shrieked into the beautiful morning. "Good-bye, you two! Good-bye!"

"You can run all you want, but I'll be right on your trail!" Denzil shouted.

Kate kept waving until she couldn't see them

anymore, until their two small dots faded into the distant landscape.

"Well, Kate," Miss Bunceton said, settling her impressive bulk into a seat. "I hope you enjoyed this little excursion."

"I really did, Miss Bunceton."

"And that something made some kind of impression — "

Kate touched her lips with her fingertips. "At least two things, Miss Bunceton."

"Good. I was so afraid you'd find this trip boring, Kate. I *hope* you weren't bored most of the time."

Kate snuggled down into her seat, shaking her head. "Not most of the time."

"Maybe you can put it all in a story, dear. A good writer saves everything up here," Miss Bunceton tapped her head, "and uses it to create."

"Maybe I will. Maybe I'll make a whole project out of it."

"Splendid. Such as?"

"Oh . . . a western horror novel?"

"Good heavens, for a minute I thought you were *serious*!"

Kate leaned against the windowpane and smiled.

About the Author

RICHIE TANKERSLEY CUSICK was born and raised in New Orleans, Louisiana. She has been a writer of songs and literature since she graduated from the University of Southwestern Louisiana. Like Kate, she has attended several writers' conferences herself, but so far has been fortunate enough to escape with her life!

Ms. Cusick is also the best-selling author of the Point paperbacks *April Fools*, *Trick or Treat*, and *The Lifeguard*. She currently lives outside Kansas City, Missouri, with her husband, Rick, and her cocker spaniel, Hannah.